Eagles' Rest

John Eagles was tired. After ten years of constant travel, living by his wits and his gun, he wanted to retire and live at peace. This was why he was heading home, back to his family and his old name of Adler. He expected to see some change, but not as much as he found.

Why was someone hired to kill him before he even got there? Where had the small farms and ranches gone? What had happened to his family? Who were the three drifters who kept crossing his path? John could have just ridden on through and settled somewhere else, but he was determined to stick it out until the mysteries were solved and find the rest he so desperately needed.

Eagles' Rest

D.E. Jeffery

A Black Horse Western

ROBERT HALE · LONDON

© D.E. Jeffery 2014
First published in Great Britain 2014

ISBN 978-0-7198-1179-1

Robert Hale Limited
Clerkenwell House
Clerkenwell Green
London EC1R 0HT

www.halebooks.com

Falkirk Council	
Askews & Holts	2014
AF	£13.75

Typeset by
Derek Doyle & Associates, Shaw Heath
Printed and bound in Great Britain by
CPI Antony Rowe, Chippenham and Eastbourne

CHAPTER ONE

The road to Diablo wound uphill through the scrubby desert, a mere trace of brown in a yellow, seared edging. The pervading dust hung like a shroud and the flies were everywhere. It was a tired road that seemed unending; a mere passage to nowhere. At this point it paused at a flat crown of wasteland, the only saving grace of which was a pool of scummy water, the ideal environment for rattlers, flies and other pestilential nuisances. The weekly stage-coach made a brief stop here to rest the horses and let the passengers and crew stretch their legs after the long haul through the desert.

Here was the spot Greg Dooley had chosen, overlooking the pool. He lay, belly down, in a group of rocks and scrub that gave him a clear view along the road and across the green coated water. His rifle lay on the ground, close at hand, and he was sweating like a pig. God! It was hot. Hotter than he'd ever known it. The flies were a constant irritation, settling on his unprotected face and sipping the sweat from his skin. He flapped them away with one podgy hand and cursed his luck.

Where the hell was the stage?. Never the most punctual of services it was late even by the company's own erratic timetable. Then he thought of the money he was owed for doing this job and smiled. Just one shot and he would be rich. A snake slid past his left hand and he froze in panic. God! He hated snakes, you could never tell where the bastards would be. He watched it slither away to descend the hill before him and began to breathe easier. Dooley settled down again and looked out over the sparse scenery. There was movement in the water as a lizard slid across the surface and vanished into the grass at the edge. The silence was getting to him and he was beginning to get very impatient. He would certainly have earned his money; if the heat and flies didn't drive him mad the silence would. It was just as he sank deeper into self pity that he heard it.

Very faintly, he could hear the sounds of the approaching coach. The groan of badly greased wheels, the pounding of hoofs, cries of the driver and gasping of weary beasts, accompanied by a cloud of dust, heralded its appearance. Gently sliding his rifle into position Dooley clicked a shell home and pulled the butt into his shoulder. His eyes settled on the sights as he prepared to carry out his task. With a dull squeal of brakes and grunting of tired horses, the vehicle drew to a halt. Dooley focused on the door and ignored the men unharnessing the beasts and leading them to the water. His finger tightened on the trigger as the door opened and the first passenger descended. This proved to be a corpulent figure dressed like a dude with top hat and fancy vest, who gingerly placed one foot before another on the uneven ground. The second person to exit excited Dooley more. She was a beauty and he looked forward to making her acquaintance when this job was done. After all, he would have dollars jingling in his jeans and what woman could ignore that? He licked his lips in anticipation. Oh Glory! He would enjoy that. He brought his attention back to the job in hand. A young man with the appearance of a drummer leaped nimbly from the carriage and looked for some praise from the lady. Dooley was pleased to see that she ignored him. He peered down and could clearly see that the coach was empty. His heart sank, the man he was looking for wasn't there. He cursed aloud and relaxed his grip on the rifle. What the hell had happened?

He heard no sound of approaching feet, sensed no other presence nearby but suddenly felt something cold and hard against his left ear. A soft voice warned him not to move and he saw a hand reach over and remove his rifle.

'Stand up slowly,' the voice continued, 'and tell me who you were looking for.' Dooley obeyed, there was no real alternative. The pressure of the gun barrel was taken away from his ear but he knew that it would still be pointing in his direction.

For the first time he saw his visitor; a small man, neat and well built, tanned and smiling although the eyes remained cold. The barrel of a Colt was aimed directly at his heart and didn't look likely to move. Above all he noted the man's dress: black jeans, black vest and cherry-red shirt. This was the man he had been ordered to kill.

Something must have registered on his face because

the other man's smile became broader.

'Surely it couldn't have been little ol' me?' he chided. 'Don't tell me that someone paid you to bushwhack a humble traveller who is doing no one any harm. Do you know who I am?'

Dooley nodded. 'You're Johnny Eagles,' he stammered.

The man nodded. 'Right. And your name is. . . ?'

'Greg Dooley,' came the reluctant reply.

Eagles nodded in satisfaction. 'That's better. I like to know who I'm gonna kill. It tidies things up. Now, Greg Dooley, who paid you to kill me? Time is passing and I'm not a patient man. Names and reasons please. Pronto.'

Dooley blustered, now terribly afraid.

'I don't know whose idea it was. Some stranger in a bar asked me if I wanted to earn a hundred dollars and I said sure, who wouldn't?'

'Who indeed?' agreed Eagles 'Carry on.'

'They told me you'd be on this stage and they wanted me to shoot you.'

'And you wanted the honour of killing Johnny Eagles, is that it?'

Dooley nodded and Eagles pondered awhile as he gazed at his captive. Finally he spoke.

'I don't like bushwhackers,' he muttered. 'Them and bounty hunters are just about as low as you can get. However, I've decided not to kill you, this time. I just want you to drop your gunbelt, leave your rifle on the ground and skedaddle before I change my mind. A few words of warning before you do: I suggest that you keep out of my sight; I could have a rethink. *Sabe?*'

Dooley nodded and dropped his belt as requested. He turned towards where his horse was tethered but Eagles' voice stopped him.

'I don't think you should ride away, you could turn back on me. Exercise will do you good. March!'

Dooley glowered but did as directed and began walking.

'Mr Dooley,' Eagles called, 'you may need this.' Dooley turned in time to catch the water bottle he was tossed. 'Have a nice walk.' Eagles turned away and watched the stage-driver reharnessing his horses. Dooley sensed that Eagles' attention had shifted and slyly drew a vicious looking knife from beneath his collar. Holding the blade between his fingers, he eyed Eagles' unprotected back. He never knew where the dog came from; there was just a growl and screaming agony as it tore out his throat.

The sound roused Eagles and he turned to see the dog lying over the dead bushwhacker. He noticed the knife and guessed what had happened. He patted the dog's head and spoke to it gently.

'You've done it again, old pal. I guess I owe you one more. Some people you jest can't help. Come on, boy, let's bury this carrion and see what Diablo has to offer.' The hound lifted his blooded muzzle and almost grinned its agreement.

CHAPTER TWO

John Eagles took time to bury Dooley's body and cover it with a small, stone cairn to discourage scavengers. Job completed, he mounted his horse and followed the trail taken by the departed stage. Leading the dead man's horse and with the dog ranging beside him, he followed the trail back to the town he had left so many years ago.

He rode slowly, enjoying the quiet company of his silent companions. There was no great hurry and, as he rode, he drank in the long forgotten sights passing his eyes. Memories of a bygone life, one he had almost forgotten, invaded his mind; days of childhood, of wonder and a quest for knowledge; days of his youth, long departed.

The desert was changing now, the dust was becoming less as the grey scrub gave way to healthier-looking grass and bushes. Birds were appearing and their song began to fill the air. The sun, in its huge blue blanket of sky, lit up the distant mountains and silvered their crests. These were the mountains that had intrigued him as a boy, the ones that had lured him away from his home and family into an adventurous life and a reputation he had never sought. The same mountains, once filled with mystery, were now old acquaintances. His dreams had been many and the solitude of the mountains had given him the peace he sought. Now they were like old friends welcoming him back. As he looked he saw the widespread wings of the eagle which had called to him and had given him his new name.

On he rode and saw many familiar sights: the eyes of a cottontail staring at him from its sanctuary in the undergrowth, the sinister shape of the coyote slinking through the brush, a mother quail busily escorting chicks across the road before him. Suddenly he saw his mother's eyes on the day he left home. She had pleaded with him to stay but his father had told her to let him go.

'Your boy is a dreamer,' he stated. 'He has to work it out of his system. Let him drift. He'll come back soon enough, when all his dreaming's done.'

Well, now he was back. He wondered how much had changed. Time had altered him, he guessed that it would have changed everybody else as well Ah well! He'd find out soon enough.

He rode on into the setting sun and finally reached the little town called Diablo. He smiled when he saw the dog turn off the trail and disappear into the brush. John grinned, the animal was never one to seek human company. Now he turned his attention back to the town of his childhood. There wasn't much to distinguish it from any other town he had ridden into during his years of travel: the same dusty streets which would turn to mud during the rains, the same clapboard buildings, each with its own false face of glory. One saloon, several stores and the hotel decorated the main street with the wooden church blocking off the end, causing a branch away to the east and where it had all started so many years ago.

He reined in outside the hotel and swung from the saddle. As he tethered the horses and shouldered his saddle-bags, he was aware of eyes watching him; something else he had grown used to over the years. During that time he had developed an instinct for danger which had kept him alive; that same instinct which had warned him of Dooley's presence earlier. Now he sensed no immediate danger and felt free to enter the hotel.

It took time for his eyes to adapt from the bright sunlight of the street. A man was behind the bar which served as a reception desk. The desk clerk looked up from his contemplation of the dust to see who was invading his privacy. John crossed the floor and requested a room. The clerk reached under his ponderous belly and pulled out a grimy book from under the desk. He handed this to the visitor and growled, 'Make your mark in here.' John picked up a nearby pencil and signed with a flourish. The clerk looked amazed.

'Don't get too many drifters who can write,' he muttered. 'How long you staying?'

'Let's say a couple a days,' the visitor replied. 'Depends how welcome this town makes me.'

The desk clerk grunted and handed his guest a key. 'Top of the stairs, door on the left,' he announced. 'You'll have to carry your own duds up. Ain't got no fancy bellhops.'

John grinned. 'Do you have a livery service?' he asked.

The other man nodded. 'Sure do.' He called over his shoulder, 'Jobo, out here and tend to the gentleman's hoss. Come on, he ain't got all day.' A tousled-haired boy emerged from the back and eagerly ran over to the visitor's side.

'Hi, mister,' he cried. 'I'll tend your hoss for you. No need to fuss yourself. I'm the best man for hosses round here. When you're settled I'll take you round to him. OK?'

'Seems good to me,' John smiled. 'He's the bay. Don't touch the grey, he belongs to another feller. I'll tend to him later.' Jobo smiled and dashed out of the door. John could hear the sound of hoofs as his horse was led away. He picked up his saddle-pack and walked towards the stairs. The voice of the clerk stopped him.

'A dollar in advance will hold the room for you.'

The man in the red shirt pulled a coin from his pocket and tossed it over to where the desk clerk caught it and thrust it into a drawer in the desk. John climbed the stairs and entered his room. which was fairly typical of the time, A chipped and scratched cupboard with a few nails for hangers served as a wardrobe. A wash hand basin, jug of cold water and a bed. Even the solitary chair looked tired and drab. Not much but it would do for a while. The hotel was new to him, it had been a hardware store when he'd left. He raised the bedclothes and looked carefully. No sign of unwelcome guests in the bedding. Good! He hated pants rabbits and he'd had his share in his life.

Laying down his bundle he crossed to the wash basin and looked in the mirror. The cracked glass revealed a

13

dark, tired face with weary brown eyes peeping out from the bushy brows. He needed a shave, but that would have to wait 'til morning, the barber's shop wouldn't be open this late. For now he needed a wash and a meal. Splashing the cold water from the jug into the bowl he removed his upper clothing and washed off the worst of the trail dust. His mind was working furiously on the same question. Who had hired Dooley to kill him? How did anyone know he was heading for Diablo? He hadn't known himself until that day.. It was a mystery he was going to have to solve and pretty damn quick before that same someone tried again.

Refreshed and dressed he wandered down into the hotel foyer. The same fat man was behind the desk and John crossed over to him. The desk clerk seemed more affable this time. Why the change?

'Where's the best place for a meal?' John asked. 'I know it's kinda late.'

The fat man smiled. 'Mrs Larriby is the woman you want. Widder woman, lives just down the street a piece. Does a real good steak. Say Will Hardie sent you.'

The visitor nodded his thanks and Will Hardie returned to contemplating the dust on his desk.

CHAPTER THREE

Out in the main street dusk was settling in and life was beginning to stir in the saloon which cast its light onto the dusty road. The main business of the evening had yet to begin: gambling, music and laughter would come along later. For now the newcomer enjoyed the relative peace.

He rode Dooley's grey round to the sheriff's office. That building hadn't changed. There was a fresh shingle on the door stating that the lawman in possession was one Chet Gower. John hitched his steed and entered. A rangy, black-haired man was seated behind a desk and looked up at the intrusion. John wasted no time, he'd been down this track before.

'I'm John Eagles,' he stated boldly. 'If there is any reason you want me out of town let me hear it now. It'll save a lot of trouble.'

The sheriff raised his brows. 'Should there be any problem?' he asked. 'As far as I know there is no warrant out for you and, as far as I'm concerned, you can stay here as long as you like. I know your reputation, of

15

course, but so long as you don't start any trouble we will get along great.'

John nodded; he was going to like this man. 'I don't plan on starting anything but other folk may have different ideas. Someone hired a feller to kill me on the way here. I didn't kill him, but a friend of mine did when he tried to knife me in the back. Does that go against me?'

Gower scratched his dark chin.

'Not if that's the way it was,' he said. 'Do you know the name of the bushwhacker?' John nodded.

'Greg Dooley,' he replied. 'I've got his horse outside.' Gower gaped and then, to the visitor's surprise, he burst into uncontrollable laughter. The gunfighter watched in amazement until the sheriff finally regained control and wiped his streaming eyes. He looked at his visitor and apologized.

'I'm sorry, but the idea of anyone hiring a no-count like Dooley as an assassin is so funny. He was probably the worst shot west of the Pecos. If he aimed at a barn door he'd probably miss the whole building. Did he give you any idea of the fool who hired him?'

John shook his head; more puzzled than ever.

'Anyway,' Gower continued. 'No one is gonna be too upset at his passing. He was just a useless drunk. The only surprise is that he lasted this long without getting his fool head blown off. You can expect no trouble on his account. I'll take care of his horse later. Now, where are you headed for tonight?'

The Widow Larriby's place was easily found and the small, grey-haired lady bustled him into a seat at one of

the quartet of tables that graced the spotless floor. The
table was covered with a gingham cloth and a small vase
of flowers decorated the centre of it. John removed his
hat and looked at his surroundings.

'Purty place you have here, ma'am,' he remarked.
'Right purty. I hope Mr Hardie's recommendation was
correct. He tells me you do a real good steak with all the
trimmings. I'd like to order one if you please.'

The old lady blushed girlishly. 'Don't take too much
notice of what Will Hardie says,' she stated. 'He talks a
little too much for his own good. I'll rustle you up a meal
in no time at all. Would you like coffee while you're
waiting?'

'That'd be fine and dandy,' responded the visitor.

She bustled away and hurried back with a huge coffee
pot and a mug. Eagles sipped the steaming brew and
smacked his lips.

'If the meal is half as good as this it will be great,' he
stated. She blushed again and went off to finish his meal.
John leaned back and lit a cigarette. He was not a regular
smoker but sometimes it helped him relax. It also helped
him think and his mind came back to the same questions. Who and why?

His thoughts were broken by the entrance of three
more men, cowboys by the look of them. They sat at a
nearby table and resumed their conversation. Clearly
they were arguing over something in that jocular way
men who knew and respected their companions often
do. The big one was leading forth.

'I ain't never seen Hickok or Earp but the fastest man
I ever saw was the Pecos Kid. Pure sheet lightning he was.

17

I've seen him clear leather before the other guy touched his gun butt.'

One of his companions, a younger man scoffed. 'Pecos Kid, phooey. Where is he now?'

His companion looked sheepish as he replied. 'He's dead.'

'Yeah! Shot down by Wyatt Earp. He couldn't have been that fast, could he?' He laughed triumphantly and turned to the third man for acknowledgement. This man, willow thin with a sad face, enhanced by his drooping moustache, paid no attention. His gaze was fixed firmly on the man seated across the room. His companions suddenly noticed this lack of attention and followed his gaze. All they saw was a small man, dressed in black except for a cherry red shirt. Just another drifter, nothing special. The thin man spoke softly, anxious not to rouse the attention of his co-diner.

'Keep it to yourselves, *compadres*, but if you are talking about fast draws you should look carefully at the *hombre* sitting over there. I'm telling you that he is a man you don't annoy.'

'Him?' The big man was astonished. 'He don't look too much to me. He's just a little runt. He don't even look like a fighter.'

'Don't let looks fool you,' the other man continued. 'I was in Tucson when he was challenged by four gunfighters. I'm telling you he killed the lot and they only got two shots off between them. His name is John Eagles.'

'Yeah?' The giant was scornful. 'I don't believe a little feller like that can be so dangerous. I've heard of Johnny Eagles, who hasn't? But I'll bet you a dollar that ain't him.'

'I'll take some of that,' his skinny friend cried and they spat on their palm and smacked hands together. 'How do you intend to find out?'

'I'll walk across and ask him,' the doubter stated. Skinny looked doubtful.

'Be careful, Carl,' he warned. 'There are probably only two fast men left alive: I'm one and he's the other. Someday we'll have to settle who is the fastest. One thing is sure, he's too fast for you.'

The big man sneered, rose from his chair and crossed to the man in question, who eyed him from under drooped lids. The intruder came straight to the point.

'Hey, feller, my sidekick over there reckons your name is Eagles. That right?'

'People who I don't know call me Mr Eagles,' came the reply.

The big man grinned. 'My name is Carl Lewing,' he stated. 'Now we are interduced I repeat my question: are you John Eagles?'

The little man looked at him and drawled, 'I am John Eagles. Now, can I ask you a question? What damned business is it of yours?'

Lewing puffed up and winked at his colleagues.

'Mr Bones over there reckons as how you are the fastest gun he's ever seen. Is that right?'

'I don't know what gunmen he's seen.' John was losing interest, his eyes were on the kitchen as he awaited his steak. Lewing persisted.

'Claims he saw you in Tucson, where you killed four men.'

'Possible.'

19

'Maybe you could show us just how fast you are, just so we can compare.'

John rose to his feet, his eyes were cold and Lewing began to feel uncertain, his confidence sinking. The gunman's face remained calm as he spoke quietly.

'I ain't in the habit of showing off, or drawing my guns lightly. I don't go in for exhibitions or competitions. If I draw my gun it means I intend to use it. So if you want to see how fast I am, call me out and see if I am faster than you. *Sabe?*'

Lewing swallowed hard, trying not to lose face as he returned to his seat. His friends tried to josh him but he remained quiet and quelled. Finally he signalled to his companions and all three men left the room. John sat down and enjoyed a really fine meal. Hardie had been correct: the steak was one of the best he'd ever sampled. After paying, he left the widow's establishment and wandered back to the hotel. He paused briefly at the livery stable and found his horse in better condition than he had seen it for many a day, coat shining, eyes bright and belly full of fresh hay. He reminded himself to praise the kid. What was his name? Jobo! He certainly knew his job. Tomorrow was the time to return to his past, tonight he needed sleep.

The room was more comfortable than he expected, the mattress had been changed for a newer one and was soft enough to relax even the most restless soul. Habit insisted that he check the room for dangers and, before unbuckling his gunbelt, he wedged a chair against the door handle. Anyone entering would make a noise and alert him. He looked out of the window and could see no overlooking windows where a gunman could lurk. As far as he could tell the room was as safe as he could make it. None the less he removed his belt and kept his gun close at hand as he lay on the bed. His mind kept working and he tried to think of what he had learned that day. The sheriff seemed OK, not the bombastic type he had met before, The big drifter in Ms Larriby's posed no real threat, but the thin man with him caused some thoughts to run around in John's head. Something about him was threatening, as though he was a form of Nemesis he would meet later on. The second mystery was who would hire a useless gunman like Dooley to kill him? Or maybe the intention was to warn him not to come back to Diablo. That seemed more likely.

He turned his mind towards tomorrow. After he had shaved and had his haircut he would ride out to the old place and see how his folks were. He hadn't realized just how much he'd missed them. Pa, big loud and hard-working who expected his sons to be the same. Soft, gentle, golden-haired Ma: he remembered the tears in her eyes as he rode off. Tomorrow he would hold her, kiss her, and say how sorry he was. Maybe even Pa would listen and forgive him. Then there was his sister, Laura. God, she must be woman by now; there were probably a whole pack of young men trying to court her. Pa would be keeping a close eye on that.

Tomorrow. Tomorrow there was so much to do, but tonight he drifted off to sleep.

CHAPTER FOUR

The morning sun burst through the window to wake him from a sounder slumber than he had enjoyed for many a day. His employment did not give him much time for true relaxation, one of the reasons why he would have to quit. Ten years was a long time for a professional gunfighter to last. He'd been lucky, he'd admit that, but how long would Dame Fortune smile on him? Maybe people would learn to leave him alone here, but yesterday, in the dining hall, didn't show that it was likely. That fool cowboy could have pulled on him and then the whole thing would start again. He'd be fine if people would just let him be.

He swung his legs off the bed, rubbed his eyes and washed the sleep and sweat from his body. He pulled on a clean shirt and jeans and ran his hands through his hair. Two priorities then, breakfast and haircut. Let's see what the old place had to offer.

Mrs Larriby's breakfast of ham and eggs, served with copious amounts of of strong, black coffee made him feel like a new man. The widow woman wasn't around, a young girl, tall and blonde, was serving today. She smiled at him in a shy way and reddened each time he spoke to her. Leaving his money on the table he wandered out in search of a barber shop.

Memory led him and he was pleasantly surprised to see that the old familiar building was still there. Furthermore the barber was still Henry Cantrell; older, greyer but still the same man he had known as a kid. For a while he stood and gazed through the window but eventually opened the door and entered.

Henry didn't look up at his new customer's entry, just carried on shaving the man in the chair. His razor strokes were as certain as ever, age hadn't caused his hands to tremble. He washed the razor and closed it. He placed a hot towel over his customer's face and, at last, looked in the younger man's direction.

'What can I do for you, son?' he asked, not recognizing the stranger. John reflected that it had been ten years.

'Just a haircut and shave please, Henry. The way you used to do it.' The barber stood stock still, realization dawning slowly. He blinked his eyes and stared harder.

'Well, I'll be darned! It can't be. . . Not after all this time.'

John's grin grew wider. 'Here I am, large as life, twice as ugly, and if you don't remove that towel your customer will be steamed to death.'

Henry reacted and pulled away the towel from the man's face who was rather red but otherwise unhurt. The barber gave the man another towel to wipe himself with and took his money. The customer, with a last glare at

John, stomped from the shop. Henry shrugged and turned his attention to the younger man. He extended his hand and smiled, John shook, and moved over to the chair.

'Good to see you back, son,' Cantrell said. 'I've been hearing about things you've been doing.'

John grinned wryly. 'Some of them may even be true,' he remarked.

The old man picked up his scissors and began cutting. 'I can't say how sorry I was to see you leave here when you did,' he began. 'It was all unnecessary. Why couldn't you stay?'

John looked mildly surprised. 'They were going to hang me,' he stated. 'I thought that was reason enough. When a lynch mob, led by your own father, is on your trail you don't hang around.'

Henry nodded sadly. 'It only took two days to clear that up. Your father was sick as hell when he realized what he'd almost done. He tried to find you but no one knew where you were. You'd just disappeared.'

'Anyways that's all over now. I'm back and I mean to stay; if folks will let me.' There was a touch of sadness in the last remark which Henry chose to ignore. It was none of his business after all.

'I guess you came back for the wedding,' Henry said, trying to brighten the atmosphere. 'Should be quite a shindig. Everyone's looking forward to it.'

'What wedding?' asked John.

'You mean you don't know?' Cantrill gasped, looking surprised. 'Young Laura is getting hitched on Thanksgiving Day. Thought you knew, what with coming

24

back and all.'

'No,' confessed the customer. 'I didn't know. Married? She is only a kid.'

'She's eighteen,' the barber corrected him. 'And right purty too.'

'My baby sister,' the young man mused. 'Where will I find her? Out at the homestead?'

'Guess she'll be in the schoolhouse right now.' mused the barber. 'Her being the school ma'am and all.'

John nodded and thanked the man. Haircut and shave done he left the parlour and wandered off towards the old schoolhouse. It didn't take too long and gave him time to see just how the town had grown in ten years. The railway hadn't reached here yet, maybe it never would. Diablo didn't amount to a heap of dust and offered nothing to the wide world. He noticed that Doc Slavin still had his shingle on the wall; good old Doc, always a family friend. Several buildings had sprung up and the town had grown slightly to cater for the increased trade from the cattle ranches just to the south, where the grass had grown thicker as it moved away from the barren north.

A few ladies were gathered on one corner, idly chatting as ladies do; a couple of old-timers sat enjoying the sun and chewing their baccy. No one paid him any heed and that was how he liked it.

The schoolhouse was quiet, kids still studying in their classes. John leaned against the fence and memories flooded back. Old Parson Hammond with his strict rules and liberal application of a birch cane for the awkward ones. John recalled the sharp sting of his punishments, ever the rebel, but he'd learned. Mrs Evans, quiet, calm and always ready to lend a friendly shoulder. All gone now, dead before he left the place. Changes, many changes. He wondered if he should have come back, but then this was his final chance to end it where it had all begun.

The sudden ringing of the old bell told him that it was play time. All hell broke loose as the yard was suddenly invaded by dozens of children, girls and boys, large and small; milling, squabbling, shouting and squealing. He grinned as he saw the small figure at the top of the stairway. The years had changed her: she was no longer the scrawny, spindly-legged girl he remembered, she was now a beauty. Her ash blonde hair flowed luxuriantly down her back to the slender waist. The white dress showed every outline of her tender young figure. Someone was a lucky man. She turned to re-enter the building and he picked his way across the playground, dodging the curious kids on the way. She went into one of the rooms and he followed. Unaware of his presence she began to clean the blackboard. He kept his voice soft as he spoke her name.

'Hello, Laura, it's been a long time.'

She whirled, startled by the voice and stared at her visitor. Recognition came slowly, he saw it dawn in her blue eyes.

'Good Lord! It can't be! It isn't. . . .'

'I think it is,' he grinned.

'John! Oh my God, John! You don't know how good it is to see you after all these years. Her hand flew to her mouth, her eyes remained wide. Suddenly she threw caution to the winds and hurled herself into his arms, raining kisses on his dark face. Neither of them heard a third person enter until a voice interrupted their joy. Laura broke away from John's arms and faced the new arrival. Her brother turned too and saw a tall, rangy figure standing, hand on hips and glaring at them.

'Can anyone join in?' the sheriff growled and Laura grabbed Eagles by the hand and pulled him towards the angry man.

'John,' she began, 'I want you to meet my future husband, Chet Gower. Chet, this is my brother, John.'

The sheriff looked at the other man. 'Mr Eagles and I have met,' he said. 'I never knew you had a brother. You've never mentioned him.'

They shook hands and retained their grip whilst both men assessed each other. Both could define characters from handshakes and neither man saw any weakness in the other. The lawman spoke first.

'You are full of surprises, Mr Eagles. Anything else I should know about?'

'None that I know of,' the other man replied. 'I left here a long time ago and we never kept in touch. It wasn't until Henry Cantrell in the barber shop told me about the wedding that I realized that Laura was still here.'

John looked at Chet and two pairs of eyes locked. One pair dark brown and one pair blue, they met and a spark of trust and friendship sprang between them. Laura saw the signs and smiled. The two men in her life were going to be friends and that put everything right with her.

John grinned and remarked, 'I guess I should ride out

27

to the old place tomorrow, see how the old folks are getting on. Maybe by now Pa will have forgiven me.' Laura's smile left her lips and she gazed helplessly up at the lanky sheriff. Gower looked awkward and coughed.

'You mean you don't know?' he asked. Laura turned her eyes back to John. A soft, hurt look marred the blueness of them. Eagles realized just how like Mom she was.

'We couldn't reach you; we had no idea where you were. So we couldn't tell you.'

John was worried now and found himself getting impatient. 'Tell me what?' he cried.

Gower cleared his throat. 'There ain't no easy way to tell you, friend: your parents are dead.' The shock hit like a hammer blow. Dead? Both of them? They weren't old, so how had it happened? Gower continued, 'Your ma caught a fever about two years after you left. Doc Slavin did his best but there was nothing anyone could do. The doc was the only one who kept your pa going after that; he seemed to just fall apart. Then, about a year later he found your pa sitting under an old oak, with a carbine barrel in his mouth. Looked like he'd had enough and just blown his brains out.'

John looked up, puzzled.

'Pa would never have done that. He was a deeply religious man and never owned a gun in his life That was part of the reason for the arguments between us. He hated guns.'

Laura walked over and placed her hand on his shoulder. Her eyes were full of tears and John realized that he too had not forgotten how to cry.

'Grief can make people do strange things,' she murmured. 'He missed Mom and you terribly. He never quite recovered from the day you rode away.'

Her brother sighed and wiped his eyes.

'I didn't have much choice,' he muttered. 'I was facing a lynch mob, or thought I was, I didn't want to end up hanging from a branch of the nearest tree.'

'They soon sorted that out,' she replied. 'Even Doc Slavin has forgiven you. He knows you didn't do it.'

'I didn't know that,' muttered John. 'I'll call in at his surgery and explain things.'

'You won't find him in there,' explained the sheriff. 'He quit as doctor some while back. He lives way out of town now and we don't see much of him. The new doctor has just started out and hasn't changed the shingle yet. You'll met Slavin when he's ready.'

'Ride out and see the homestead anyway,' suggested Laura. 'Old Eli will be glad to see you.'

'Eli?' gasped John. 'Is that old maverick still around? He must be eighty by now.'

'And he's still as cantankerous as ever,' smiled Laura. 'I've got to go now, boys. Unlike you two I've got work to do. Come round to my place tonight. I'll cook you a meal.'

Her brother pulled a face. 'I've tried your cooking before, Sis, and I've only just recovered.' He ducked as a stick of chalk whistled past his ears and Gower ushered him out as the girl flounced away.

'She has changed a lot lately,' the sheriff whispered. 'She takes a pride in her cooking and, to be fair, she is pretty good. I've put on a few pounds since I've been

with her. Come over tonight and find out for yourself.'
He patted his flat belly and John grinned.

'How did you two meet?' he asked. 'I can't imagine my
baby sister as some feller's wife. I can only imagine the
skinny nuisance I grew up with.'

Gower grinned ruefully. 'Losing her folks like that
made her grow up, I guess. When I first saw her I thought
I'd never seen any woman so sad. I guess she took a shine
to me. Don't know why. Could be my handsome face and
manly body, it don't much matter. Whatever the reason
we got on well together and she learned to smile again.'

'It seems I owe you a lot of thanks,' John remarked.
'She sure seems happy now and that's the main thing.
Just make sure she stays that way or her big brother will
come after you.'

'No danger of that then,' Gower grinned. 'I ain't planning to upset her too often. She has one hell of a temper
on her.'

John grinned, slapped the sheriff on the shoulder and
together they walked back into town.

CHAPTER FIVE

They parted at the sheriff's office and John made his way back to the livery stable where he found his horse was being tended by the kid. He was pleased to find Jobo giving the beast a good brushing. Its coat was gleaming, eyes bright, it looked completely refreshed. The boy looked up as he saw the gunman and his smile nearly split his round face.

'Hi, Mr Eagles,' he called. 'I'm just finishing off. He sure is a great looking horse you got here. What's his name?'

The man rubbed his chin and looked mildly puzzled as he replied. 'Well, what do you know? I've never got round to asking him. He's just horse to me and I guess I'm just man to him.'

The boy looked astonished. Everyone he knew had names for their animals.

'You mean you've never named him?' he gasped.

John shook his head. 'We don't talk a lot so the idea never arose. We just plod along as pals. We've been together for about four years, I guess, and no one ever complained.'

Jobo grinned. It was rather pointless, he guessed, naming animals.

'Mr Eagles' – his voice was hesitant; the man said nothing, let him find his own way – 'could you do something for me? I'll pay you, I have a few dollars salted away. I ain't no freeloader.'

John smiled, he liked this kid. 'There ain't no need to talk about payment, son. Not among friends. I hope we are friends.'

Jobo's smile grew even broader. He spoke quickly, the words just gushing out.

'Can you teach me to be a great gunfighter, like you?'

John looked down into the eager face. The blue eyes and broad smile spoke of innocence, full of young dreams. He sighed, vaguely remembering when he had been at that stage. What the hell had gone wrong? He picked his words carefully, eager not to burst the kid's bubble.

'I can teach you to use a gun,' he began, carefully. 'I can teach you all I know about the care of guns. I could teach you to be the fastest draw in the West, but I won't. If you're going down my path I'd try to stop you. There ain't no future in gunfighting. I've spent ten years of my life just trying to stay alive. I can't walk down any street and not be looking for some jasper who will suddenly spring from the shadows, just trying to prove he's better than me. I've been ordered out of near every place I've been to just because I might start trouble. Well, Jobo, I can say that I've never started trouble anywhere, but when you build up a reputation you just can't stay still. No, son, I won't teach you to be a great gunfighter. I'd like you to live long enough to enjoy your grandchildren.'

The boy looked disappointed. His dreams were not going to be fulfilled by this man. He tried a different tack.

'You've survived though, ain't you? You're still around. That must prove something.'

John smiled, a sad smile, no hint of real mirth in his dark face.

'It proves I've been lucky. Someday my luck'll run out and I'll be just another tombstone on Boot Hill. Everyone will forget me because some other fool will take on the role. Now my offer still stands: I'll teach you all I know about guns, caring for them, choosing them, firing them, but I won't make you into a gunfighter. Now is that a deal?' The boy nodded and John grinned his approval.

'Have you got a gun?' Jobo shook his head. 'It helps to have one, but we can start with mine.' He passed over his Colt and the boy gripped it eagerly. 'Now how does it feel?' the man asked.

'It feels sorta heavy,' Jobo confessed. John nodded.

'That's because it isn't the right gun for you. Do you know how to open it?'

Jobo nodded and cracked open the cylinder.

'Good! That's a start. Now empty the shells.'

Jobo obeyed but had to ask. 'Why? I can't fire a gun if it ain't loaded.'

'Exactly,' the gunfighter replied. 'We're sitting in a barn; you've never fired a gun in your life and I'm feeling unsafe. Now, how many shells did you take out?'

'Five,' announced the boy.

'But this is a six-shooter; why are there only five bullets loaded?'

'Dunno.'

'You should always keep one cylinder empty because if your hammer is resting on a live shell all the time you could get into a situation where the trigger is knocked and you shoot your own foot off. *Sabe?*' Jobo nodded. The two of them spent the next hour exploring all aspects of the gun. Jobo learned how to strip it, clean it, oil it, reassemble and load it. He learned most things to do with a gun but he didn't fire it. John wound up the session by saying clearly what he considered to be a few basic facts.

'You can use a gun for many things. You can bang a nail in with it, hit someone over the head; stir your coffee with the barrel, but it's only made for one purpose: it's made to kill. Without a gun strapped to your waist you can live a perfectly normal life; strap on a gun and you are fair play for any jasper who fancies his chances. If you're prepared to carry a gun you must be prepared to use it. Finally never pull a gun in anger. Rage can make you careless and that can kill you. Understand? Good! That's all for today. Another day we'll pick a gun for you and start a little target practice. Oh, there is one more thing before we stop. Can I have my gun back please?' Jobo grinned and handed the weapon back. John checked and reloaded it.

He smiled to himself as he walked from the stables. He liked Jobo, the kid reminded him of what he used to be; eager as a puppy, keen to learn and a good handler of horses. He only hoped the boy would follow a different path. His own life was the sort he wished on no one. He was just turning towards Main Street when his name was called.

'Adler, John Adler. It is you, isn't it?' John turned towards the source of the voice. He recognized the small, spare figure looming before him. The long hair and beard were greyer and the eyes a little more rheumy but he was still the same old man.

'Doc Slavin,' he greeted. 'You're almost right. I'm Eagles now, John Eagles.'

The old man snorted. 'Don't matter two bits what you call yourself; you're still the murdering bastard who killed my son.'

The younger man tried to keep calm. 'That was an accident,' he retorted. 'Burt was three years younger than me and twice as stupid. There were three of us there, your other two sons and me firing at an old can when Burt decided to dash in front of us. We all fired at the same time. I don't know which shot killed him and neither do you.'

The doctor's face turned purple with rage.

'Pity you didn't stay to plead your case. You ran off from the posse.'

'That wasn't a posse: it was a lynch mob, and I'd have been strung from that tree before I could have explained anything. A lynch mob, and you were at the head of it.' He was getting riled now. 'Was it you that hired that back shooter to gun me down on my way here?' Slavin looked astonished.

'I don't know anything about that. Why would I hire a gunslinger when I have two sons ready to come for you?

35

When you die, Adler, I want to see it. I want to see your life's blood pouring out like my son's. I wouldn't want you to die away from my sight. I only live to see that happen then I can quit this life a happy man.'

He spat in the dust and turned away. John stood for a while, just thinking. Had he made a mistake coming here? There must be other people than the Slavins who still hated him. But who had set up that trap along the trail? Why would someone hire a gunman as inept as Dooley to do the job? Maybe they didn't want him dead, maybe they wanted to rouse his curiosity, to ensure that he took up the challenge and come back to Diablo. Ah well! It was too deep a mystery for now. Tomorrow he'd select a gun for Jobo; for now he had a dinner in the old homestead to look forward to. A good meal, in congenial company, what more could a man ask for? He turned back into the stable and told Jobo that he wanted his horse and the boy rushed to fetch saddle and harness. He swung into the saddle and, with a farewell wave to the boy, who was happily clutching a silver dollar, he rode out of town towards the hills and home.

CHAPTER SIX

He wondered if it was wise to visit the old place where his childhood had been spent, the farm where he'd caused so much grief and disappointment to his father. He'd wasted so much time dreaming. He recalled the hours of work neglected and abandoned to his dreams. The mountains had always called him and, despite all his efforts, they posed a constant attraction Those same mountains he was riding through now, only this time they were crying a welcome home to him. He remembered Ma's tears and Pa's whippings that had not altered him at all. He could hear Pa's words after one such beating.

'I guess I'm wasting my time, boy, you are just a dreamer, good for nothing until you get this wanderlust out of your fool head. You can hear the mountains calling and you'd better listen to them. Follow your heart and come back when you are settled and feel like doing some real work.'

Well, he'd finally come back and it was too late. He couldn't take Ma into his arms and tell her how sorry he was: he'd never hear that big booming laugh of his father. Will, his younger brother, had died before he left, now there was only Laura and she was passing into the care of another man. He liked Chet Gower, figured he would take good care of her, but so many changes were too much for him.

He pulled up at the gate, uncertain of what to expect and whistled in surprise. The little place sparkled in the sun, everything neat and gleaming. The chickens were fat and healthy, the small plots of vegetables and fruit were well tended. How did Laura run this place and still work at the school? He lifted his hat and scratched his head. One black strand of hair blew across his eyes and he brushed it back as he replaced his Stetson. Respect for his sister grew; what a woman she had grown into.

Leaning from his saddle he opened the gate. He urged his horse forward but changed his mind when a gunshot sounded and dust spurted up from between his horse's hoofs. A voice called from somewhere in the house.

'That's far enough, mister. You ain't gittin' no nearer 'til you state your business, and maybe not even then.'

John grinned, after all these years the old fool was as feisty as ever. He called back, 'Come on, Eli, stop playing games. What happened to that good old Southern hospitality you used to brag about?'

There was a pause and then the reply. 'Hospitality died when I was left to run this place by myself. How the hell do you know my name?'

'I'm getting tired of this. You are Eli Thompson and I used to be John Adler. Now can I come in?'

'John Adler?' the voice was showing signs of doubt. 'Mr John left here years ago and ain't expected back. Can you prove you're an Adler? What were the names of your ma and pa?'

John let his grin grow wider, he couldn't blame the old fool for being careful: a black man alone in a white man's house could get into trouble easy.

'My father was Thomas Henry Adler, my ma was Ellen Milburn Adler, my brother was William Henry Adler and my sister is Laura Ellen Adler. Anything else you want to know?'

'You could have read the gravestones before you reached the gate.' Eli was consistent if a little unsure. John shook his head.

'The graveyard is round the back and Laura's name won't be on it because last time I saw her she was fit and well and planning her wedding. Can I come in now?'

After a pause a figure emerged from the darkness of the barn and, rifle still trained on his visitor, advanced towards the gate. He hadn't changed much, still the same small, wiry figure, a little stooped with snow in his hair. He peered at John like a man whose sight was failing and suddenly gave a wild whoop of pleasure.

'Jesus H. Christ!' he howled. 'It is you. I'd recognize that ugly mug anyplace. Master John as I live and breathe. Glory be! There are still miracles. Why are you sitting there like that? Come in and have a cup of coffee.' At last John was at home.

The old man ushered him into the house, poured coffee and began a potted history of the last ten years, the words flooding from his mouth like a waterfall.

'Hey, steady on, old-timer.' John stopped him in mid flow. 'Just a little at a time. Maybe it would be better if we just asked each other questions. That way we both have a chance. Now, who's been running this place since Pa died? I expected it to be run down without his hand on the reins. I was surprised when I saw how good it was looking.'

Eli scratched his head and grinned. 'Miss Laura did her best, but it was too much for a lady to handle so I offered to help. At first there was three of us, Luke, Joel and me but the others drifted away after a time and me and Miss Laura took it on. I know she don't make a living out of it so I agreed to work for my keep. It suits us jest fine.'

John shook his head in disbelief. This man must be working every hour of daylight, he deserved some form of payment.

'Eli,' he began, 'I don't know what to say. I've a little money stashed away and as soon as I get my hands on it I'll pay you your back wages. That's a promise.'

Eli rose to his feet, anger on his face as he glared at his visitor.

'I ain't taking no money from you or nobody,' he snapped. 'My deal is with Miss Laura. I'm well fed, got a roof over my head and a job I like. What would I do with money? Money is for spending and if I went into town with coins jingling in my pocket I'd be jest an uppity black and someone would find a way to take it from me. No siree, Mr John, you keep your money, you need it more than me.'

'But that doesn't seem fair,' protested John.

The old black man sniffed. 'Life ain't fair,' he grumbled. 'Was it fair that some white man up north should set me free? He never asked me about it. That meant that hundreds of slaves, just like me, lost the only homes we knew. We had no jobs. Who'd pay a black man when he could use a white man? The white folk never accepted us. We even have different laws. A white man can do what he likes to a black gal, but if a black man looks the wrong way at a white woman they hang him. Is that fair? Don't talk to me about being fair. Jest leave things the way they are and we'll all be happy. Right now I've got to go see to the cows. I'll see you again before you go.' With a nod of his head he left the room.

John sat and sipped his coffee, he had no idea the old man had such strong views. He'd clearly been away too long.

Finishing his coffee he rose and made for the door. Wandering around the back of the house he found the family burial plot. Once there was only one grave, now there were three. Three stone crosses with names carved on them, stark and cold in the warm sun. The centre one was dedicated to his mother and memories came flooding back. A gentle woman with that core of steel so necessary in a frontier wife. Her soft exterior didn't stop her from being able to control some of the excesses in her three headstrong men. Father had always listened to her, she was the one with the sense. John remembered her tears as she begged him to stay, knowing it was useless: the hills were calling her son and he had to go.

His gaze shifted to Pa's grave. More memories swam back. A big man with a quick temper. He remembered the whippings again and glanced at the mountains. The call was gone, his dreaming over, and it was too late to shake Pa by the hand and say sorry. He lowered his eyes and looked at the third grave: Will's. The younger brother who was everything John wasn't. A born farmer, he tackled every task with an energy that John secretly envied. He worked like a beaver to do John's work as well as his own to protect his older sibling from their father's wrath. It was this that had killed him. The two were attempting to repair the barn roof. Will was working and John dreaming when it happened. John heard the cracking of timber and snapped to attention too late. Will disappeared through the hole which had appeared and impaled himself on a metal spike on the floor of the barn. By the time John got down to him he was dead. Tom Adler was very quiet from that day, he never said a word to John, just let him suffer his own feelings of guilt. Their relationship changed. John was accepted as being around but that was all. Tom only spoke to him when he had to and John's sorrow grew heavier. That was when his departure became inevitable.

His memories were broken into by a soft voice.

'Bring back memories, John?'

He turned to find Laura at his side. She smiled and took his hand. As the wind ruffled her golden hair he was suddenly struck by how much she resembled their mother: the same gentle, calm smile and bright blue Milburn eyes totally unlike those of her father and brothers.

'I was just thinking about the great condition the old place is in. You must have worked like the devil to keep it up.'

She smiled. 'It was tough at first,' she admitted, 'But Eli decided to stay. He is great with the farm work and the animals. Then I met Chet and he pitched in with general upkeep, leaving me to handle the woman's side of things. When we are married he will move into here and resign as sheriff. Now you are back the four of us can really make a go of it. You are staying, aren't you?'

'I guess so. I ain't got nowhere else to go. I ran out of dreams a long time ago. I've seen oceans and great ships; I've ridden through deserts, prairies, mountains and forests; I've lived through heat, snow and blizzards. There isn't much left.'

She looked deeply into his eyes. 'You sound bitter, John.'

He shook his head in denial. 'I'm not bitter. Just a little tired and lonely. I just want to settle down and quit running. I really want to relax, if only folk will let me. Guess I must be getting old.'

'You need a good woman behind you,' she suggested. 'Have you never thought of getting married?'

He grinned ruefully. 'There was a girl once, a long time ago, but now it's too late.'

'It's never too late, John. Your chance will come again.'

'There'll never be another Nita.' John's voice was flat, cold, lost in the past. 'She was something different. I was working for a rancher in Tucson at the time. Wrangling horses, breaking 'em and such. She lived in the town, working as a dressmaker and doing pretty well. She was just about the loveliest thing I'd ever seen. It took me a long time to speak to her. She sort of tied my tongue up

43

and I stammered like a school kid when I tried to talk to her. I guess I must have looked kinda stupid and then she asked me to take her to the dance. She said later that if she had waited for me to ask her we would both have been eighty before anything happened.' He smiled ruefully. 'I guess she was right.'

Laura broke a short silence. 'Did you take her to the dance?'

'I sure did and it was one of the best nights of my life. She made herself easy to talk too and we stayed together all evening. Things went great from there and we even fixed our wedding day. God! I was a happy man.'

'But something went wrong?' Laura was full of concern for her big brother. He swallowed hard and she could see tears in his eyes now. She instinctively touched his arm.

'You could say that. Something called the Hennesseys. They were a work shy pile of dirt not worthy to walk in her shadow. There were three of them and they had been pestering Nita for some time but she kept fending them off. They didn't take kindly to our relationship but didn't have the guts to do anything while I was around. A week before our wedding I had to go off and bring in some wild mustangs, an easy job that wouldn't take long. But it was long enough for them. They broke into Nita's home and had their fun with her. They raped her, cut her throat and left her to bleed to death. I came back home expecting a wedding and got a funeral.'

Now it was Laura's turn to cry. She clutched her brother's arm and wept. Finally, through a veil of tears she asked, 'Did nobody help her? She must have screamed.'

'No one cared, she was only a Mexican and they only rate slightly higher than a black. It was down to me to do something. That's the only time I've killed in anger. Usually it's just a job, but this time it was different. I made sure that all three of them died slowly, in pain, but I knew that their pain was less than Nita's had been. That was when I knew that love was not for me. Nita was all I ever wanted. My last tribute to her was to always wear a red shirt. She made me my first one. She liked me in red and I've worn one ever since. Always with my initials 'J.E.' on the pocket. That's my story, Sis, sorry it ain't a pretty one.'

Laura reached up and gently kissed his cheek. 'It's all over now, John. You're back home where you belong. We can run this place together, the four of us. Chet will be quitting as sheriff soon, we will be getting married and moving into Ma and Pa's old room. Yours is still waiting for you if you want it. Why not join us, John? We can be a family again. You've been drifting for ten years now, you need to settle down. Why not settle here?'

John thought about her words. They made sense, but was she right? He certainly craved a quiet life but would he ever get it? Were there too many skeletons in the closet to allow him peace? He'd tried to settle before but some jasper had always spoilt it. Maybe here, back in the Adler home, with a family, he could finally bury John Eagles and settle down as John Adler. It was worth a try.

'It makes sense, little sister,' he replied. 'Give me a while to think and I'll let you know. OK?' She nodded, aware that she could expect nothing more and they walked back home arm in arm.

CHAPTER SEVEN

It was a small cabin, just a battered old shack really, two bedrooms and a main living room with a cooking area tucked away in the corner. This consisted of a dirty pot-bellied stove and a wash basin. It was no luxurious abode but it suited the group of people assembled. Doc Slavin was holding court, pacing the dirt floor while the others looked on. Slavin was not happy.

'After all these years why did he have to come back? Just when everything was going great he had to appear. Am I ever gonna get rid of this itch in my flesh? These damn Adlers! Just when you think you are winning another turns up. Someone is gonna have to get rid of him, but who is man enough for the job?'

It was the thin man who answered his question.

'You ain't giving us an easy job,' he drawled. 'I've seen this man in action. He was using the name Eagles then, John Eagles. He is just about the fastest man I've ever seen. When he goes for that gun he is pretty nigh unbeatable. It'll cost more than you've been paying to tackle him.'

The big man with him snorted.

'Horse feathers! There ain't no one that fast. I've met

the jasper and he was just a little runt of a guy. Nothing to be afraid of.'

Bones grinned. 'Is that why you backed down?' he said.

Carl's face reddened. 'I didn't back down,' he denied. 'I just wasn't ready. I'll have him next time.'

'Let me know when you are ready,' Bones sneered, 'I'd sure hate to miss it.'

One of the other men butted in now, a younger man with the sharp features and big nose of Doc Slavin.

'I can't see what John Adler has to do with anything. Why should his turning up make any difference?'

The Doc snorted in disgust. 'Have I got to remind you that it was Adler who shot your brother Burt? Has it slipped whatever passes for a brain in your head that this murdering scum is still walking the streets while Burt rots in his grave? I won't rest until the whole pestilential family is under the sod.'

The rest of them looked at each other while the Doc paced the floor.

'I bred three sons, three to help me fight the Adlers and what did I get? One is in his grave and the rest are as useful as a dead coyote. All I asked Brett to do was court the Adler girl and get her to marry him; that way we would have got their place for nothing, but you let that scrawny sheriff take her away from you. Just like her mother, she's a two-timing bitch. As for you, Calvin, my first born, I got you a job with the railroad so you could gather information for me and you got yourself fired for stealing something completely useless. That sums you both up, completely useless.'

The brothers looked at each other and reddened,

their attempts at explaining their failures ignored.

The doc continued. 'If no one can come up with better answers and damned quick I suggest you all get out of my sight and let me think for myself.'

Calvin grinned and stood up. 'Don't go worrying none about John Adler, Pa, I've arranged a little surprise for him. He ain't gonna be around to bother you much longer. Trust me, his hash is settled.'

The doc cast his eyes to heaven and cried, 'Oh my God! Why does that statement fill me with worry? Get out of my sight, the lot of you.'

The others looked at each other and walked out, the two brothers walking together.

Outside Brett grabbed his brother by the sleeve and asked, eagerly, 'What have you got planned, Cal? Will it really make Pa happy?'

'He will be happier than a rabbit in a cabbage patch, jest wait and see,' Calvin said.

Brett had to be satisfied with that. His brother, however hadn't finished.

'Whatever happens it's got to be better than your idea, sending a no account like Dooley to ambush him. What was he gonna do, talk him to death?'

Brett's lips tightened. 'John Adler was my friend, I didn't want him dead. I just wanted to scare him off, change his mind about coming here.'

'That worked well, didn't it?' Calvin grinned nastily. 'All you did was stir him up. My way Adler will be dead soon and we can settle down again.'

The younger man had to make do with that.

CHAPTER EIGHT

The meal was splendid, chicken cooked in a spicy sauce with mounds of potatoes and beans, cooked just the way John liked it. Both men leaned back in their chairs and belched in unison, which brought a smile to all three faces, although Laura tried to look disapproving.

'That was a right fine meal, Sis,' John congratulated her.

She curtseyed gracefully and murmured, 'Thank you very kindly, sir, but it isn't over yet. Do you boys reckon you could manage a slice of apple pie?'

Gower loosened his belt. 'I might just be able to fit that in, honey. I've always managed to before. How about you, John?'

'Reckon I can rise to the challenge,' the other man replied. 'Wheel it in, Laura, and let's see what damage we can do to it.' The girl smiled and retreated to the kitchen to emerge with a huge pie the smell of which made their mouths water.

The three made short work of the delicious pie, largely due to the contented efforts of the two men. Dishes cleared away they both sat still until Laura joined them. The sheriff spoke first.

'I was telling your brother what little I knew about the local events, your folks dying and all. I am only a recent settler here, drifted in about two years ago. The old sheriff stood down and I was the only candidate so I got the job. Met Laura and that's about all I can tell you.'

John nodded and switched his attention to his sister sitting quietly across the table from them.

'Tell me about Ma and Pa, Sis. Chet has told me they died. Pa was supposed to have shot himself, but I can't believe it. What can you tell me?'

Tears formed in her eyes as she replied, 'After you left, Pa continued to rant for a while. You were a complete disgrace, a gun-toting no-good who would never amount to anything. Even when he learned the truth, he refused to forgive you. You know what he was like, John, deeply religious, he couldn't cope with the fact that you had killed someone.'

'It was an accident,' her brother cried. 'There were three of us kids having a shooting competition. As we drew and fired at the old can on a tree stump Burt ran in front of us. None of us had a chance to hold back, it was all too quick. Any of the three shots could have killed him. I was the oldest and took the blame. I had to leave town in a hurry because Doc Slavin whipped up a lynch mob. They weren't gonna listen to anything I was going to say. That's the honest truth, Laura. The most hurtful thing was that Pa believed them and not me. I rode away, changed my name and tried to start again. I thought I could, but when I came back and met Doc Slavin I realized that it hadn't been forgotten.'

'The truth came out later when a little boy told what had happened,' whispered Laura. 'He was watching from the brush. Your name was cleared, but some people never forgot. Especially the Slavins. Calvin and Brett have both vowed to kill you when they get a chance.'

'Watch out for them, John,' Gower muttered. 'They ain't quick shooters but they are mean. They wouldn't worry about back shooting if necessary.'

'Thanks, Sheriff, I'll be on my guard,' John nodded. 'Now, tell me about how my folks died.'

'Ma never got over losing you and couldn't understand Pa's attitude. She just sort of faded away. That was about three years after you left. The shock turned Pa's mind somehow. He was never the same man. He began a religious crusade, condemning almost everyone with some kind of sin or another. He began trying to shut the saloons as dens of iniquity, brothels filled with fornicators and harlots. No one was safe from his sharp tongue. Then, one day, he was found up in the hills, he'd blown his brains out.' The tears were flowing now and Gower crossed to her side. She buried her face in his chest. John allowed her time to recover before he spoke.

'I guess the Slavins have got a lot to answer for. It ain't easy carrying a grudge that long. I still can't believe that Pa would shoot himself, he hated guns too much. His mind must have turned real bad to do that. All this happened and I knew nothing about it.'

'We couldn't find you. No one knew where you were. We heard reports of John Eagles but didn't realize that it was you they were talking about.'

'I guess it was my fault for going off like that. Anyway

that's all over now. You are about to start a new life with this feller holding you close. The way I see it you'll have a great life with a good man and a hatful of kids. I hope I'm getting an invite to the wedding.'

'You're getting more than that,' Laura smiled. 'I'm hoping you will take Pa's place and lead me down the aisle.'

John was staggered and his mouth dropped in surprise. It was some moments before he replied.

'Miss Laura Adler, I would be honoured.'

CHAPTER NINE

He rode slowly back towards town, still thinking about Laura's offer. It was certainly tempting but would it be possible or would it just bring trouble down on those he loved? Ten years of looking over his shoulder, constantly watching for some back shooter to turn up when least expected, for some jasper eager to make a name for himself, had built a wall between him and normal folk. Of the Earp brothers only Wyatt was alive, Hickock had gone, what chance did he stand? Someday, somewhere, his turn would come. Was it wise to involve Laura?

He was still pondering when the sound of gunshots came to his ears. His instinct took over and he flung himself from the saddle and, gun in hand, listened. The shots continued but were some distance off in the trees. He crept forward using all available cover until he reached a break in the undergrowth which led to a small clearing. This dipped down to a shallow gully and he could see a small figure busy reloading the gun which he and John had selected earlier in the day. John grinned and stayed silent as Jobo aimed at a can perched on a tree stump some distance away from him. He aimed and fired in one fluid movement but narrowly missed his target. Two more shots had the same result and John crept closer. The boy lowered his weapon in frustration and a little imp of mischief touched the gunman's lips. In one rapid burst he fired three times. Jobo leaped to his feet while the can whirled and twisted as the three shells struck it. The boy spun round and relaxed as he saw John holding a smoking gun.

'Holy Moses,' he gasped, 'how did you do that?'

John's grin grew wider as he replied, 'Just lucky, I guess. You didn't do too bad; you just didn't allow for the kick, is all. Here, let me show you.'

They spent the next ten minutes or so working to improve the boy's skills until John called a halt.

'It's getting kinda late now, son. Get on your horse, I'll ride home with you.'

John's mood had lifted; this boy was good for him. Maybe he would stay after all. Perhaps it could work out.

CHAPTER TEN

John walked through the darkening Diablo main street feeling happier than he had for many years, almost as happy as when he had been with Nita. That pain was still there although the bitterness and hatred had faded. Now his kid sister was finding her own happiness and it was rubbing off on him. He thought of the deaths of his parents and regretted the fact that he hadn't seen them before they went. He especially rued the way his father had died. Something was wrong there, but he couldn't figure out what. His attention was lacking its normal alertness so he didn't see the dark shape that slipped down an alley ahead of him. He walked on, lost in his reflections, when a sound reached his ear. A soft, metallic click, all too familiar to him, The sound of a gun being cocked. He was now fully alert.

His eyes moved although his head remained in the same position. To an onlooker he was still lost in thought, but he was now in full awareness and at his most dangerous. He caught the glimpse of a reflecting metal in the dark alley to his left and his muscles bunched ready for action. He could now see the faint shape of the rifle barrel being raised, and timed it perfectly. As the weapon flashed he fell to the left, his gun leaping into his right hand, barking out death. The rifle bullet whistled past his cheek and a cry came from the alley. As he hit the dirt he saw another figure fall forward from the shadows and land in the dust. After a few minutes the figure had made no movement, John rose to his feet and moved forward cautiously. There was no need for caution: his adversary was dead.

A small crowd was gathering, it didn't take long for vultures to appear, thought John. One man was already shouting his mouth off.

'I saw it all,' he proclaimed. 'This here feller was walking along, minding his own beeswax, when the other man tried to gun him down from the alley. Jesus H. Christ! I never saw anybody move that fast. He was just like lightning. Whoosh! Bang! It was all over. Jesus H. Christ!'

The sheriff pushed his way through the gathering crowd to lean over John and the body.

'You OK, John?' he asked 'What happened?'

'Pretty much what that guy back there said,' replied the other. 'I caught a gleam of his rifle barrel in the alley and reacted. I was lucky, I guess. Do you know him, Chet?'

The sheriff shook his head. 'Stranger to me,' he murmured. 'Anyone know him?'

'He was drinking in Mikey's place,' someone replied. 'Really hitting the whiskey bottle.'

The sheriff searched through the dead man's pockets

and found a wad of notes.

'This'll do to bury him,' he remarked, 'the rest can go to the town funds. It'll help pay my wages. Now, is there anything else in his other pockets?' He rummaged through and came out with a crumpled piece of paper. He unrolled it and whistled as he read the words on it. Without speaking he handed the document to John who found he was looking at a wanted poster. The picture was a close resemblance to the dead man and the wording read:

WANTED
DEAD OR ALIVE
ARTHUR P. HOLBORN
REWARD
$200

The sheriff cleared his throat and stated.

'You've earned yourself a tidy sum of money, John. I'll get the paperwork sorted and get the money through to you.' To his surprise the other man shook his head.

'Put that money to a good cause, the church or the school, something like that. I ain't gonna touch it.'

'But you've earned it,' Chet insisted but John again shook his head.

'If I take that money it makes me no better than a bounty hunter and I don't reckon I want to go that way. I earn my money but not by being judge and jury. My mind don't work like that.'

'If that's the way you want it, but it don't seem right to me. I know the school needs money to build a few more rooms so I'll give the money to Laura, she'll handle it.'

The small man nodded his satisfaction. 'The main problem now is who's the jasper who's trying to kill me? There have been two attempts so far and I don't want there to be a third. It's time I got it sorted out.'

'That's my job,' stated the sheriff.

'You do what you can, Chet, but it's getting kinda personal and I'm not going to rely just on you. I'm gonna use my own methods.'

'Just keep it legal, John, I don't want to go against you for many reasons, but mainly Laura.'

'You won't have any worries on that count,' John said, and turned away to continue his journey to the hotel.

He arrived back at his room and tossed his hat onto the bed. His mind was in a whirl. Two attempts on his life in two days. Why? He could see no reason for it. Who had he upset? The Slavins? Not their style. Bullies they may be, vengeful certainly, but they'd do their own fighting, not hire others to do it. So who? Apart from them folks had been welcoming. True he hadn't met too many people yet but there didn't seem to be any real reason for hating him apart from the Slavins.

He unfastened his gunbelt and looked around the room. Nothing had changed. He crossed to the window and looked out onto the street. Just the usual early evening traffic. In the middle distance he could see the undertaker's wagon where they were busy removing the body. Life was returning to normal, saloons were livening up, the cat house shone its lights across the main street and he could see the sheriff beginning his rounds.

John turned back to his room and flung himself on his

bed. He was beginning to regret coming back home, folks had warned him that it never paid. He cursed himself for a stupid fool and then thought about Laura. It had been great seeing her again. She seemed to have picked a pretty good man as a husband, Chet Gower looked a straight enough feller, he'd look after her. He let his thoughts drift back to the past, to Nita, and what might have been. They had been full of plans but the Hennesseys had finished those. He kicked his mind back to the present but not before a tear had forced it's way from his right eye. Must it always be like this? Would he never find peace?

CHAPTER ELEVEN

He woke suddenly. There had been no intention of sleeping but somehow it had happened. A cold feeling of dread crept over him. He didn't like lapses like that; in his profession he couldn't afford. them. Anything could have happened. He gazed around the room, nothing looked different. Maybe he could breathe a sigh of relief.

He swung his legs off the bed and rose to his feet. The only light in the room was coming through the dirty window and he went to look out. Diablo was coming to life, music and laughter from the saloons and squealing from the cathouse. The dark clad figure of the preacher strode the street crying his words against sedition and debauchery. His accusations of fornication went unheeded, most of the people in earshot didn't know what they meant anyway. John turned away with a smile and picked up his hat. He suddenly felt thirsty and decided that a beer would be in order. He had enjoyed his time with Laura and Chet but now he felt he wanted to meet fresh faces, maybe renew old acquaintances.

The saloon was smoke filled and crowded as he pushed through the doors. A few men were seated around the local cardsharp, playing poker, more were swinging their glasses and singing more or less in time with the piano. Some were gathered along the bar and John recognized the three cowboys he had met in Mrs Larriby's the previous evening. The big one, Carl, was holding forth.

'I don't believe any of those tales about fast guns and gunfighters. All stuff fit for dime magazines and such. Show me a gunfighter and I'll show you a blowhard.' He paused as he caught sight of the newcomer. The memories of their previous encounter still rankled. He leaned an elbow on the bar and watched as John caught the barman's eye.

'Beer, please.' John spoke quietly and Carl grinned. He signalled to the barkeep who began to look very worried.

'There's a tradition in this bar,' the big man began, 'all strangers are greeted with a welcome drink from the townsfolk. Since you are the only stranger here, Mr Eagles, I guess that rule applies to you.'

John looked at him and smiled. 'Am I the only stranger here?' he asked. 'Everybody is a stranger to me; but thanking you kindly, I'll buy my own drink.'

Carl frowned and ignored him.

'Give the gentleman a whiskey,' he instructed the barman.

The glass was filled and pushed before John who pushed it to one side saying, 'I don't have a taste for whiskey.'

Carl pulled his gun and pointed it at the other man's head.

'Drink it,' he cried. John shrugged, complied and pulled away coughing and spluttering.

Carl turned away laughing loudly. 'Gunfighters!' he roared. 'All blowhards.'

His laughter stopped as a glass of milk was pushed in front of him. The other man spoke quite quietly. 'I'm returning the favour. Drink it.' This command was backed by a cold gun barrel which was thrust into Carl's ear. He decided to comply. John holstered his weapon and said, 'We are all square now, I guess.'

Carl's huge fist struck a powerful blow and the gun-fighter fell flat and unconscious on the floor.

'We are now,' the big man growled, and turned back to his companions. He was just beginning to get his boasting back into full flow when the chair hit him across the back of the head and he knew no more.

John dropped the remaining part of the chair and drank his beer. Tossing a few coins on the counter he said, 'That'll pay for the beer, milk and chair. The whiskey is on him.'

He walked from the bar and wandered out into the darkening street.

The two remaining drifters looked down at their fallen companion until the younger man spoke.

'What'll we do with Carl, Bones?'

'He looks kinda cosy to me.' his companion shrugged. 'Let him just sleep on a piece, it may straighten his brains a bit.' He pulled up a chair and sat, the boy, after some hesitation, following his example. Life in the bar resumed its usual pattern as the two men sat and drank quietly.

The skinny one, Bones, was in a reflective mood as he spoke to the boy.

'Let me tell you something, Sandy, it could just save your life. When an older man, with lots of experience, tells you something, take note of it. I told our sleeping friend there just what Eagles was like and he took no notice. He's lucky he's still alive. Twice he's crossed swords with Eagles and twice he's come out still breathing. It won't happen that way a third time. There's no way that Carl is ever gonna outdraw John Eagles. He just hasn't got that edge. Now, if I recall rightly, it's his turn to buy a drink. Just take the money out of his poke and pay the barman what he owes.' Then, as the boy rose to comply, he added, 'Don't forget the whiskey and the chair. There ain't no reason why the saloon should suffer for Carl's foolishness.'

CHAPTER TWELVE

Back in the stable John found Jobo busy with the horses. He stood watching for some time before the boy noticed him. Jobo pulled back from his task and sighed contentedly as he surveyed his work. Something drew his attention to the quiet man standing in the corner watching. He gave a start of surprise and then relaxed when he recognized his visitor. The now well-known grin did its face splitting act and he gave his attention to his new friend.

'Gee willikins, Mr Eagles. I never heard you coming. How long you been there?'

'Long enough to see what a great way you have with horses,' replied John, smiling. 'It's a skill not too many people know. How'd you learn it?'

The boy blushed with pleasure.

'Grew up with horses, I guess. My pa used to train and break horses for the army. They were always around the place and folks reckoned I'm half horse myself.'

John laughed; he liked this kid.

'Where is your pa now? he asked.

A cloud moved over the boy's face and John felt sorry he'd asked, but Jobo eventually replied, 'He died with Custer at the Little Big Horn. I was just a little button then but folks told me he died a hero. That made things seem better. Since then I've lived and breathed horses. There didn't seem much else to do, until you came along.'

John began to hear warning voices in his head, he didn't like the way this was going.

'What do you mean?' he asked.

The boy looked down at his feet, embarrassment oozing from his every pore.

'I hoped you could make me a great gunfighter like you, then I can earn a living by killing the bad guys for money like you do.'

John's voice grew sharper now and his eyes hardened.

'Is that really what you think I am?' he growled. 'A hired killer who goes around killing the "bad guys"? Well, let me put you right. I've occasionally acted as a lawman and killed men in the line of duty, but generally my killings have been in an honest effort to stay alive. I get my money by working, same as you. I've been a horse wrangler, cattle drover, scout, guide and hunter. I've never had the divine power to distinguish who are "good guys" or "bad guys" so now we've got things straight on that count, if you want to stay my friend, you'll quit that kind of talk. Understand?' The boy nodded, chastened, and John instantly softened his approach.

'Now, if you still want to learn how to handle a gun properly, I'll help you. Is that OK?' Jobo nodded and John sat on a hay bale and signalled the boy to sit beside him.

'Right, *compadre*, let's get going. I saw you practising with that new gun we picked. How did it feel?'

'Great!' the boy exclaimed.

'It looked good and you were doing pretty well when I saw you, but there was one thing you did wrong. Can you guess what it was?' Jobo shook his head and John looked at him before replying.

'You were trying to be too fast,' he answered. 'Before you can run you've gotta learn to walk. Just practise your aim first, then, when you can hit the target five times out of six, try drawing and aiming. As you get better, speed up. It may take months, maybe years, but it's the only way I know. Have you cleaned your gun since firing it? No? Then let's clean our weapons together. They've both been used and ought to be looked after.'

The boy eagerly began stripping down his gun and John, slightly more slowly, followed his example.

They worked in silence. A kind of friendship was developing here; John could feel it. Finally he spoke.

'How'd you get the name Jobo and why don't you go to school like other kids your age?'

The boy looked up. 'My folks called me John Junior but that got shortened to John Boy and then Jobo. It just sorter worked out. Now everybody calls me Jobo. I quit school when my pa died, got myself a job so that I could help my ma. Schooling don't seem that important when you can earn money. I can read and add up my pay so what more do I need?' His face was hidden from John's view but his voice was breaking with emotion. This kid was missing out on a lot of growing up time. John placed his hand on the boy's shoulder and squeezed it gently.

'You certainly know horses,' he remarked. 'You can get good work along those lines. People always need good horses.'

'Maybe even one like you've got,' he exclaimed. 'That's just about the finest piece of horse flesh I've ever seen. Where'd you get him?'

'I won him in a card game in Tucson,' John grinned. 'He was just a colt then, wild as the wind and twice as strong. It took a long time to tame him, but now we are long travelling old friends. We know each other so well you'd think we were brothers. If ever anything happened to me I'd want him to go to a right good owner, someone to look after and understand him. Someone like you.'

The boy's eyes popped open and he gasped, momentarily lost for words. 'Do you mean that, Mr Eagles? Honest? A horse like that for me? Wow!'

John rose to his feet and grinned down at the boy.

'Don't go getting any ideas now, I aim to live a while yet so don't plan to shoot me for him. I won't appreciate that.' With that final crack he walked out of the stable still grinning.

CHAPTER THIRTEEN

The next morning he found the sheriff in his office ploughing through a mountain of papers. Gower looked up and grinned with relief as he saw who his visitor was.

'Come on in, John,' he hailed. 'Am I glad to see you.'

'I'm not interrupting, am I?' John asked.

The sheriff's grin grew wider. 'Anybody who can drag me away from paperwork is welcome. Fancy a coffee? The makings are over there, pour me a cup, will ya?'

John walked over to the boiling pot and poured two steaming mugfuls. Passing one over to Chet he sat down and sipped the other.

'When I was riding around I saw that a lot of the old ranches and farms seemed deserted and I was wondering why. Could you tell me anything about it?'

The sheriff nodded. 'They all suffered problems a while back. There was a lot of damage done, crops destroyed, barns burnt, things like that. Since they were all in hock to the bank and couldn't pay their dues, Banker Schultz called them in and took over. No one has come forward to buy them up so I guess the bank still owns them. Why d'you ask?'

'Dunno really. Just curious. Seems sorta strange that they are laying empty. Prime land like that.' John rubbed his chin in thought.

'Folks did ask questions at the time but nobody could find anything wrong, I don't even think that anyone cared too much.'

'Have you got a town map that shows all the outlying spreads? One that's easy for a lame brain like me to understand?' Chet reached over to a filing cabinet in the corner and drew out a large folded document. He blew the dust away and spread it out across a convenient table top. The two men peered at it closely.

'Which are the spreads that were sold?' John asked. Chet pulled out a pencil and circled them. There were only a few, but John could begin to see a pattern. He took the pencil from the sheriff's hand and traced his own pattern.

'Notice anything, Chet?' he asked.

The sheriff thought a while before replying, 'They seem to be marking out a route, but a route to where? All there is in that direction are the mountains and Maybeline.'

John grinned a not very pleasant grin and remarked, 'There is also Finnigan's Pass. The only easy way through the mountains.'

'What's special about either Maybeline or the pass?' mused Chet.

'I don't know,' answered his friend, 'but tomorrow I aim to find out.'

'There's one more thing I've noticed,' stated Chet.

'Your spread lies right in the middle of it. Why hasn't that been targeted?'

'That's one more question I can't answer,' he replied, shaking his head. Perhaps if I pay a visit to Maybeline I may be able to answer at least one of them.'

The sheriff nodded in agreement. 'The only thing I can think of is that the railhead is there. Could be they have a new route planned to come through Diablo?'

'That's a pretty good idea,' stated John. 'You're smarter than you look. I guess that's what my sister sees in you – it can't be your good looks.'

The sheriff glared at him and muttered, 'Get out of here before I arrest you.'

'For what?' John raised his eyebrows. 'What are you gonna charge me with?'

'I'll think of something later. Get travelling, but, John' – the other man turned back – 'be careful! Something nasty is going on.'

'I didn't realize you cared that much for my safety,' John said. 'I'm really touched.'

'Don't be,' growled Chet. 'I just don't want Laura upset. Before you go I'd like to make the journey official.' He handed John a silver deputy's star.

The two men shook hands. John saddled up and headed towards the mountains and Maybeline.

CHAPTER
FOURTEEN

He started his quest by heading towards the distant hills. Despite the years of absence it was as clear in his mind as ever. The trail was familiar and old, bitter memories came flooding back. There was the swimming hole they had played in as kids, him, Will and the Slavin boys; jumping and squealing as kids do. Here was where he learned to shoot and entered an endless competition with Brett Slavin, the middle of Doc Slavin's sons. Suddenly another memory struck him like a physical blow: the memory of firing at the very instant that Burt Slavin decided to run across in front of his gun barrel. He could see the small frame in his mind's eye, the deep, ugly wound weeping life's blood on to the grass; the fading light in Burt's eyes as he cuddled him in his arms; Doc Slavin's blind rage at the death of his youngest son, the threats, the crowd-rousing speech that had almost resulted in John being lynched from a nearby tree. The escape, running back blindly to where he was sure he would be safe, back to his own home. His father's cold fury and the look in the old man's eye that caused him to keep on running. That had been the birth of Johnny Eagles and the end of John's feelings of peace and ease. He had yearned to travel but hadn't planned it to start that way. Now he was back, for good or ill. John Eagles was sick of running; all he wanted was peace and the right to be John Adler again.

Out of nowhere the dog appeared and, after a brief spell of tail wagging in recognition, trotted beside the horse. The man grinned and looked at the animal with some relief. It had been several days since they'd met and he'd wondered if something had happened to his trail companion. It wasn't unusual for the beast to lie low, he hated towns and people. Since John had saved his life he made an exception in his case. Now they were heading out into the open prairie and that suited the dog fine.

As they travelled on there were signs of Gower's report. Empty range devoid of life and care. The grass looked rich and lush but it was evident that no cattle had grazed there for a long time. What the hell was Schultz playing at? Grazing land was at a premium so how come this was unused? Maybe the answer lay in Maybeline. As the biggest town in the area, with a rail head, there were more people to help his enquiries. With luck he could find the man he was seeking.

He rode on through those mountains that had drawn him as a kid. They'd started his yearnings for travel and now they were still here after all his journeying, and the wanderlust had finally ceased.

He camped that night near a small mountain stream

where the waters ran silver and laughing over their rocky bed. He built a fire and settled down. The dog vanished into the scrub and finally returned with a rabbit which he settled down to enjoy.

John prepared a small fire, cooked his own meal and boiled coffee. Meal over he leaned his back against a nearby tree and allowed his mind to relax. He remembered the last time he had ridden this way, through the mountains that had called him for so many years. A sixteen-year-old kid with tears in his eyes and the cries of hatred from people he had grown up with, had regarded as friends, driving him away. He remembered how he'd seen the eagle soaring in its majestic freedom; how he'd decided to save his family from disgrace by adopting the bird's name as his own. John Adler had died and John Eagles had been born on that day. Now, ten years later he had returned and nothing had really changed. There had not been much peace in his life during those years, ever on the run, looking over his shoulder. There had always been some jasper determined to be the man who killed the legend. The only hope he had had, the few moments of peace, were when he was with Nita. She swam into his memory like a phantom, a shadow from nowhere. He saw her as he had last seen her alive. Bright and lovely in the morning light. Her hair flashing its inky blue lights and those huge, blue Spanish eyes swimming with tears as she bade him farewell. Her voice was husky as she whispered, 'Please hurry back to me, John. I will be waiting for you.'

Tears filled his own eyes as he recalled the next time he had seen her. Her slender body torn and blooded, her eyes dim and lifeless and her face wearing a look of pain and fear. He'd tried to wrap the bloodied and ruined form in the remnants of her dress and watched as the undertaker took her body away. The Hennesseys had paid in full but his life had been empty from then on.

Abruptly he tore himself back to reality and considered tomorrow. He hoped that he would find the man he needed in Maybeline. It could be that his work with the railroad had ended and he had moved on. He shrugged off his doubts. If that was the case he would have to try something else. There were many trails to follow. Something would turn up.

CHAPTER FIFTEEN

High in the mountains three men sat around their own small fire and waited. The sky was slowly turning to the pink glow that heralded evening and they were beginning to become fidgety. At least two of them were, Bones was as implacable as ever.

'Fer Christ's sake!' cried Carl. 'Where the hell are they? We're sitting here, like good little boys, waiting for teacher to turn up. Why the hell don't we just sell the steers we have and split the money three ways? To hell with this mysterious mastermind and his prize dogs, let's do something.'

Bones smiled lazily as he tossed the smoking end of his cheroot spinning into the fire and watched it twist and burn.

'One reason could be that I don't intend to run for the rest of my life. Looking over your shoulder all the time can get annoying.' His voice was quiet and his eyes cold. 'Some day, Carl, that impatience of yours is gonna get you into a whole mess of trouble.'

'Maybe so, but I'll have a lot of dinero to get me out

of it,' Carl snorted.

'How much money can you spend in hell?' Bones asked. 'What do you think, kid?'

The third man, Sandy, looked uncomfortable. He shuffled his feet and stared at the ground as he spoke.

'I'm new to this game, ain't never worked like this before but I reckon that the big man has been fair by us. I've got more money in my jeans than I've ever had. He ain't let us down yet and I reckon we should wait.'

'Well said!' applauded Bones. 'I don't reckon we'll have too long to wait now anyway. I can hear hoofs approaching. About thirty minutes away.' The other two stared at each other. The sense of hearing that Bones possessed never failed to amaze them. Sandy looked at his pocket watch, it would be nice to catch the thin man out. His hopes were dashed when thirty one minutes later two riders entered the clearing: two tall, fair-haired men whose looks proclaimed them to be brothers. The three men already present only knew them as Cal and Brett who worked for a mystery man called the boss. They asked no questions so long as they were paid for their work and were paid well. The brothers climbed from their saddles and helped themselves to coffee, the late sun gleaming on their golden hair as they smiled at the trio before them.

'No problems?' Cal directed his question to Bones, the accepted leader of the trio. 'Cattle OK?'

Bones nodded. 'Safely stacked in a box canyon over that ridge,' he replied. 'Plenty of good grazing, fresh water, fattening up well.'

'Good!' Cal grunted 'We'll be moving them soon.

How many you reckon we've got?'

Bones rubbed his chin. 'With the calves and the mavericks 'bout five hundred head. Maybe more.'

'OK. Now I've got a change of job for you. Tomorrow you raid the Adler place. They ain't got much stock but you can burn a few outbuildings and enjoy yourselves in their crops. There's only an old black there. He has a ancient rifle and won't pose much of a problem to you three. Then you've got to kill John Eagles. I hear you've already met the man.'

'Nothing will give me more pleasure,' Carl leered 'That feller has ruled the roost for too long. I owe him a thing or two.'

Brett yawned. 'Don't want to know about that,' he sneered. 'The boss wants him dead and reckons you men can do it. There's a bonus for the man who does. Now, let's go down and look at those steers.'

Bones nodded and ordered Sandy to show their guests where the stolen cattle were and the three departed. Carl rose to his feet and strapped on his gun. Bones looked at him quizzically.

'Where do you think you're going?' he asked.

'You heard the orders. I'm gonna get me a black and then kill that blowhard, Eagles,' cried Carl. 'It will give me a hell of a kick to see that jasper breathing his last.'

'Whatever you say,' Bones muttered. 'Myself I would rather wait until daylight when we can see the man's face as he dies. As for Eagles, he left town earlier today, heading for the eastern mountains. We won't see him for a while. I figure we should wait until he comes back and then hit his place. It will give us more of an edge. He won't be thinking too clearly when he's all riled up. That will be the best time to get him. Now, pour me some more coffee and sit down, you're making me nervous.'

Carl's thinking process was not rapid and Bones's words churned around in his head. Finally he nodded and complied. He passed his partner a mug of coffee and squatted. 'I am gonna get to kill Eagles, ain't I. Promise me that.' Bones sipped the strong, black mixture and nodded. 'I promise you'll have first crack at him, but I can't promise the end result.'

'That's up to me,' muttered Carl. 'Jesus! I'm looking forward to it.'

Bones closed his eyes and smiled. He knew in his heart that there was only one man who was good enough to face Eagles and it wasn't Carl, but he let the matter rest for now.

CHAPTER SIXTEEN

The town of Maybeline nestled snugly under the shadow of the mountains. The desert had long vanished to be replaced by lush green grass. This was cattle country. The coming of the railroad had given rise to the stockyards which John rode past on his way in. Though empty at present the smell of cattle lingered and brought a wry smile to his lips. Memories came back of happier times in a town not unlike this one where he had planned to settle and raise a family. Suddenly he saw Nita as she had been when he went on that fatal roundup. Small, with jet hair flowing across her slender shoulders and those wonderful eyes, rich, blue Spanish eyes that shone bright with love and expectation. The way she was before the Hennesseys finished with her and threw her off like a broken doll. He realized he was crying, dragged himself back to reality and wiped his eyes on the back of a gloved hand. No time to think about the past, the present was where the problems lay.

It was early morning when he rode into town; larger

and brasher than Diablo. Most of the stores and buildings on Main Street were open for business. In front of
the saloons old men and boys were sweeping up the
remains of the previous night's festivities. A few women
were standing on corners chatting in the way women all
over the world have probably always done and always will.
On the sidewalks the few rocking chairs were occupied
by sleeping men while kids ran swooping and calling in
little groups of activity. As he rode, John read the signs
on the buildings he passed: General Store, Assay Office,
Gunsmith, Hotel, Barber, Bank and finally, Attorney-at-
Law. Here he paused and carefully read the name on the
brass plate: Zachary P. Lowcock. He smiled and dismounted. Ducking under the hitching rail he tethered
his mount. It had been fed and watered recently and
would be fine for a time. He pushed open the door and
entered.

Zach had hardly changed over the years, a little more
prosperous perhaps, a touch more weight around the
midriff but not much else. He was bending over a ledger
when John entered, his brown hair flopping across his
face. He waved a hand, without looking up, and cried,
'Be right with you, friend. Just let me check on this. Ah
yes! I thought so. The crafty old buzzard.' He marked his
place and slammed the ledger shut.

'Now, how can I help you, friend?' For the first time he
looked at his visitor. He blinked in amazement and then
leaped to his feet, hand extended in greeting. 'John
Eagles! As I live and breathe. After all this time. I thought
you were dead.'

'No such luck,' John replied. 'I'm still around to

80

pester you.'

'Pull up a chair and sit awhile,' the lawyer insisted. 'How about coffee?'

John found himself seated with a steaming mug in his hand before he knew what had happened.

'Now what brings you to this neck of the woods?' The lawyer seated himself and folded his arms across his chest. 'I hope it's something I can help you with?'

John thought awhile before replying, 'Are you still working for the railroad?'

Lowcock raised his eyebrows. 'Now and then they call me in, but things are pretty quiet at the moment. Not too many people are investing their money right now. Why do you ask? You don't want to invest, do you? You could make a lot of money out of it. Our stocks are high and will go higher.'

'Not really my game. I just wondered what your expansion plans are.'

'Heard the rumours, eh? Well, if what I'm guessing is correct you could be disappointed. We've had a change of mind.'

'Can you make that a bit clearer?' John asked 'I'm only a simple man, don't complicate things.'

The lawyer grinned. '*Simple man*': that was one expression you couldn't use about John Eagles.

'OK,' he began, 'we had planned to extend the railroad out as far as Diablo to the south but decided that it would be uneconomic. After all there isn't a great deal of profit to be made from a small place like that and there isn't much more after there. The decision was made only yesterday. They are now going westwards to meet up with the railhead at Denver. So I'm afraid your home town will be left out for a while.'

'Have you got a map of the route you would have taken to Diablo?'

'Sure have. I'll get it for you.'

The lawyer rose and crossed to a huge filing cabinet in the corner. He paused in thought for a while and then bent his length down to a lower drawer. With a paper in his hand he crossed to the table and, calling John over, he spread out a map on its surface.

'As you can see here, John, it would have largely followed the trail you must have ridden in on. Through Finnigan's Pass and straight down to Diablo. There were four ranches and homesteads in the path and the owners of these would have been very wealthy men. Only now it won't happen. Does that help you?'

John looked up into the lawyer's blue eyes. Zach stood almost a foot taller and was broadly built. Now his usually cheerful face was quizzical as he awaited his friend's reply.

'Who knew about these plans?' John asked.

'Not too many,' he stated, scratching his head. 'It never pays to get too many people riled up until there is a need. The directors and officers of the railroad, the chief engineer, myself and that's about it. Why d'you ask?'

'Because someone has been driving the owners off those ranches and buying them up for themselves. The only one left unsold is where my family live.'

'So you reckon the news was leaked to someone who thought he was on to a good thing?'

'It looks that way,' John nodded. 'Could anyone have gained the knowledge without you knowing?'

Lowcock shook his head. 'This is the only map and it's kept under lock and key in this office As you can see it's still here, safe and sound.' He paused and thought. 'Wait a minute, it's coming back now. There was a series of break-ins a while back, but nothing was stolen except a few dollars from the petty cash. We caught the man and he was fired on the spot. It didn't seem worth charging him and he was sent out of the area.'

His visitor was interested at once.

'Do you know his name?' he asked.

The lawyer shook his head. 'I didn't have much to do with it but I can find out for you. It'll take a day or so. Why not spend some time with Sarah and me? You could meet my kids. But wear some ear muffs as they can be full of questions.'

'That'd be just dandy,' John replied.

Lowcock gave John directions to his house and insisted that he spend his time with Sarah, his wife. John tried to say he would rather lodge in a hotel but the lawyer would have none of it. John knew the man well and saw no profit in argument. He compromised and suggested that he save Zach some time by looking through the files to find out the name of the dismissed man. Lowcock nodded and handed his friend a huge file bulging with papers and John wished he hadn't suggested it, paperwork was never his favourite occupation.

Time passed quickly and John became engrossed in his task, Lowcock had given the approximate dates of the business and so it didn't involve too much scratching through matters that didn't amount to much so far as John was concerned. At last he gave a cry of success and leaned back. Lowcock raised his eyes.

'Found something?' he queried.

'I think so,' John muttered. 'The name of Calvin Slavin has appeared.'

Lowcock raised his brows. 'That means nothing to me. Friend of yours?'

'It's a long story, but let's say some of the muddy waters are clearing a bit. The Slavin family were close friends of my family. Calvin's father was the town doctor until he retired. It looks like he has found himself something to do to keep him amused.'

Lowcock stretched and stood. 'I don't know about you, John, but I reckon it's quitting time as we used to say on the plantation. Let's get moving and see what Sarah has cooked up for us.'

CHAPTER SEVENTEEN

The three men reined in their horses and sat looking at the Adler property spread out before them. All looked quiet enough and Bones gave them a grin.

'Looks OK to me, boys. The school ma'am ain't at home, the sheriff is in his office and Eagles has disappeared. The only person we're likely to meet is the old man who lives here and we can handle him.'

Sandy looked nervous. 'There ain't gonna be no killing is there?' he asked. 'I didn't sign up for killing people.'

'What's the matter, kid?' Carl scoffed. 'Want your pa here to tell you what to do? If we have to kill we will and there ain't nothing you can do to stop it.'

Bones's voice rang out sharply. 'Leave the kid alone. Remember when you first started out? My God! I've never seen such a scared booby in my life. We all have to begin somewhere and if the kid doesn't want to get involved he doesn't have to. We can handle the old man and maybe killing won't come into it. Sandy, when I give you the signal you set fire to that barn over there. We'll handle everything else. OK?' The boy nodded but his eyes still held the glimmer of uncertainty. Bones signalled and they fell into Indian file and rode quietly down towards the farm.

As they approached the gate a shot rang out and Eli's voice cried to them across the yard.

'Stay right where you are. State your name and business.' The trio reined in and Bones hooked his leg across the saddle as he addressed the hidden voice.

'It's OK, friend, we are friends of Mr Eagles and have just called to speak with him. Give him a yell, we'll have our talk and be on our way.'

'He ain't here,' Eli replied. 'I ain't letting you in without his say-so. Just be on your way and leave us alone.'

Bones nodded. 'Fair enough. We'll call back later when he arrives. Be sure to tell him we called.'

He wheeled his horse and turned away, the others following in his wake. Carl was angry.

'I thought we was gonna do something, not run away from an old man with a rifle,' he grumbled. 'The big man ain't gonna like this.'

Bones stopped his horse causing the other two to stop suddenly. His face was white and there was a look in his green eyes that Carl had never seen before. They seemed to glare with hatred and spite. Carl was no coward but he was suddenly afraid. Apart from his rifle the skinny man was unarmed. Carl had never seen him with a sidearm. He was lighter and skinnier than Carl, who could have snapped him across his knee, and yet the big man knew that if he rubbed Bones up the wrong way it would be dangerous for him.

'When did you win the right to question me?' The voice was very quiet, almost a whisper, but his eyes told something different. Carl knew that he was facing death and swallowed hard.

'I ain't doing that, Bones. You're the boss, we all know that. I'm a little surprised is all.'

Bones smiled and his eyes lightened a little. 'Let's get behind that knoll over there and we will discuss things. OK?' He led them to the place indicated and they dismounted. 'Take a look at the barn and tell me what you see,' he instructed. 'Make it look casual. Don't stare.'

Sandy turned his head and peeked.

'He's just standing there looking at us. He ain't going no place by the look of him.'

'That's good. Now let me know when he goes into the barn.'

He lay back against the rock with the top of his Stetson poking up above the skyline.

'You fellers do the same, let him know we are still around. Make like we've camped here.'

They bustled about and lit a small fire so that the smoke would be visible to the watching Eli. All was quiet until Carl suddenly said, 'He's gone inside the barn.'

'Right!' Bones sprang to attention. 'Sandy, give me your hat.'

'My hat?' the youngster exclaimed.

'I want him to think that there are still three of us here. If he can see three hats moving around he won't think we're doing anything. Meanwhile, you'll be creeping round to the back of the barn and, when you hear me whistle, you're gonna set fire to the it.'

Sandy was worried. 'But he'll burn to death,' he cried.

'He won't if he's got any sense,' Bones replied. 'Most likely he'll burst out of the front door and we will have the drop on him. *Sabe?*'

Sandy grinned and gave up his hat. He set off like a rabbit sneaking through the brush towards his target. His companions watched in envy, even they could not see his passage. Finally he emerged behind the barn and began to dash down towards it. His hands were already full of dry brushwood which he began piling against the wall. Bones whistled like a whippoorwill, the boy struck a match, and flames began licking against the dried timbers of the barn. Bones lined up his rifle and waited.

Inside the barn Eli settled down and watched anxiously. He automatically distrusted strangers and these three had given him no reason to change his mind. From the narrow window he could see where they had set up camp. He saw the smoke rising from their camp-fire and three hats peered over a slight incline in front of them. So all three of them were settled for the wait. As he watched, all three hats shifted slightly as the owners changed position. Eli was not a friendly man. White men had generally not been kind to him. All his young life had been spent as a field slave and, although his master had been kind, Eli had always known that he would never be treated as an equal. The War Between the States had set him free but he found that in many ways he was less free than before. Why hadn't that white man in Washington left things alone? What the hell did Abe Lincoln know about it? Eli spat on the floor and then a smell reached his nose. It took a while to register but the crackling sound helped him realize. Fire! Something was burning. He looked over his shoulder and saw the first flames licking up the dry wall at the back of the barn. Quicker than he would have thought possible the flames spread and Eli knew that he had no alternative: he had to get out quick or roast like a chicken. His eyes went back to the window and saw that the strangers' position had changed. Now two of them were facing him with rifles pointing in his direction. An empty hat dangled from a long stick and he saw how he had been fooled. A voice boomed out across the valley.

'OK, boy! You've got a choice. You can either burn alive or throw down your gun and walk out. What's it to be?' There was really no choice. Eli had to believe these men meant what they said. Carefully he opened the barn door and threw out his old rifle. The voice taunted him further.

'Good boy! Now come out with your hands up. Remember, we've got two guns trained on you so don't do nothing stupid. *Comprende?*' Eli complied. And walked slowly out of the rapidly burning barn, the heat playing on his back and the sweat running through the tight coils of hair on his scalp.

The voice called again. 'OK, kid, come around and pick up the rifle. Be careful, he's dangerous. He can move quick for an old 'un.'

The younger man appeared and Eli guessed he was

the fire-lighter. Stooping to pick up the gun he spoke to Eli softly, 'Easy, no one is gonna hurt you.' He picked up Eli's gun and carried it off. The other two men now advanced down the hill towards their prisoner. The thin one's gun barrel never moved from Eli's chest. The old man stood rock still. Finally they stood before him and relaxed slightly. The rifle barrel was allowed to droop and Bones grinned.

'Good. Now you are being sensible. It ain't right to treat decent white folks the way you did. Pulling a gun and all. You could have got yourself into trouble doing things like that. My friend here don't like uppitty blacks, do you, Carl?'

The second man grinned but there was no humour in the smile. 'Sure don't,' he stated. 'I've met them before. Think they are as good as white folks. Just because Abe Lincoln thinks so don't make it right. What do you think?' Eli made no reply and Carl's expression changed. 'Are you ignoring me?' he snarled 'Didn't your mammy teach you any manners? I am white and you are black so that makes me the boss. *Sabe?*'

Eli was scared but tried not to show it. His silence irritated Carl even more.

'By God! I'll make you learn,' he snapped, and lashed Eli across the mouth with his open hand. Blood spurted from his lips but he remained silent. Carl hit him again and this time Eli spoke.

'Mr John ain't gonna like what you are doing,' he spluttered. 'He's gonna kill you when he finds out.'

'Maybe he ain't gonna find out,' Carl cried. 'There won't be anyone to tell him.' Thus saying he picked up the old man by his vest and carried him towards the fire. Eli struggled and fought but was helpless. Sandy tried to protest but a word from Bones stopped him. The thin man just stood and watched as Eli was thrown into the flames. Eli screamed and wriggled as the fire licked at his clothes and he managed to stagger out. Carl laughed and threw him back in again. Three times Eli escaped and three times he was thrown back until finally there was no resistance, just a blackened shape in the inferno. Bones looked at Sandy, saw the boy being violently sick and laughed.

'Come on, let's get going. Our work here is finished. Now we have to find Eagles.'

CHAPTER EIGHTEEN

Doc Slavin was ecstatic, he faced his two remaining sons and smiled. His eyes were tuned to his younger son, Brett, but he addressed them both.

'At last you've got something right,' he cried. 'We are back on track now after the glorious mess someone made before.'

Brett winced but was forced to reply in his own defence.

'Aw Pa! It wasn't my fault. Women are always fickle, you know that.'

His father sneered at him and made a mockery of his son's voice. 'OK, Pa! Leave it to me, Pa! She is crazy about me, Pa. I'll get her to marry me and we can have the Adler place for nothing. Horse feathers! She turned you down and went with that lanky sheriff. That mistake has cost our backer and us a lot of dollars. I only hope the railroad deal covers it, or I'll have your hide.' Brett lowered his eyes and said no more. His elder brother, Calvin, smiled. It did no harm to slap Brett down now and then; he was getting too cocksure. The old man turned his attention to the eldest boy now.

'Any news about John Adler?' he asked. Calvin shook his head.

'He seems to have disappeared. The three cowboys are looking out for him. Don't worry, Pa. We'll find him and kill him for you.'

'No, you won't,' snapped the doc. 'Neither of you two could handle him. Leave the killing to Bones. He is the best man for the job.'

'Bones?' Brett protested. 'But he doesn't even carry a gun. What's he gonna do, talk him to death?'

His father looked at him coldly. 'I can guarantee that when Bones straps on his guns someone is going to die. Just hope it isn't you. Now get out and find him. Before you go, how are my cattle looking?'

'They're fine, Pa,' Brett answered. 'They've dropped some calves and all of them are fat and well. We must have couple of hundred now.'

'Good!' Slavin nodded and dismissed them with a wave of his hand. Alone at last he leaned back in his chair and thought. A few more attacks on the Adler spread and they would be ready to sell, provided the twin problems of the sheriff and John Adler, or Eagles whatever he called himself. could be settled. He should be a contented man but some small maggot of doubt niggled at his mind. He tried to shuffle it off but it lingered there. He would feel better when Eagles was dead.

CHAPTER NINETEEN

John was on his way back towards Diablo. His search had been very revealing and now he had plenty to think about. He was in no hurry, his mind thought better on the trail and, as night closed in, he set up camp. As he boiled his coffee and cooked the meat he had hunted along the way, the dog joined him. They sat in silence, each deep in his own thoughts. John puzzled about the ownership of the homesteads which had been taken over by the bank; who knows what the dog was thinking? The fire crackled and the meat sizzled sending its fragrance into the dark-blue, starlit sky. The dog lifted his head and a growl began in the thick, dark throat. Eagles reached out and patted the beast's head. He made a signal with his hand and the dog slipped off into the undergrowth. The man sat still, apparently unaware of the approaching horse, but inwardly on a knife edge. The unknown rider halted and his mount snickered. John lifted his head and a voice cried out.

'Hey, Mr Eagles, is that you?'

The man relaxed. 'Come on in, Jobo, sit down and

pour yourself some coffee.'

The boy rode into the firelight and tethered his mount. He smiled as he sat down and took the mug the man offered. John gave a soft whistle and the dog reappeared, warily emerging from the scrub. Jobo whistled in admiration.

'Wow! He sure is a big feller,' he exclaimed. 'Does he belong to you?'

'We travel together from time to time,' the man explained. 'Neither of us belong to the other. We get on well so it suits us to stay as pals and, no, he hasn't got a name before you ask.'

'Is he friendly? Can I stroke him?' The boy grinned.

'You can try,' his friend. warned. 'But be careful. He doesn't always take to strangers.'

The boy held out a tentative hand and the dog sniffed it. To John's surprise the hound, usually so untrusting, licked the boy's fingers and allowed them to gently stroke his fur.

'Well, I'll be damned,' John murmured, 'He doesn't even let me do that. I bet he won't take too much of it.' The dog was true to his words. Abruptly he rose to his feet, shook himself violently and sidled off into the shadows.

'Told you so,' the man remarked.. 'You've got closer to him than anyone I know. You must be kinda special.' The boy blushed his pleasure. John threw another log on the fire and looked at his companion.

'I haven't asked you what you're doing out here this late at night. Care to tell me?'

Jobo started as he remembered his errand.

'The sheriff is looking for you. There is trouble at your place. It looks kinda serious.'

'Is Laura all right?' asked John. The boy nodded and the man relaxed slightly. Rising to his feet he doused the fire, saddled his horse and said to his companion, 'I don't know what you are doing, son, but I'm heading homewards.'

'I'm coming with you,' the boy replied. 'What about the dog?'

John shrugged. 'He'll either come or stay, it's his choice. Come if you're coming.' The pair rode out of the clearing and away into the darkening sky.

Jobo rode well, John noted, and could see for the first time that the boy was mounted on the grey that had once been owned by Dooley, the failed bushwacker. Its condition was much better than when he had last seen it and inwardly he congratulated his young companion. They rode in silence until, at last, they came upon the devastation that the three drifters had left.

CHAPTER TWENTY

The three men had also built their camp-fire and were seated around its gentle flicker. Bones lay back and gazed at the stars, Carl was picking his teeth to remove the last traces of his meal while Sandy was pacing the glen and rubbing his head in anguish.

Carl glared at him and snapped, 'For Christ's sake, sit down. You're making me nervous.'

The youngster stopped his pacing and glared back at the big man.

'I can't believe you did that,' he cried. 'How could you kill a man that way? Just keep throwing him into a burning building. It was inhuman.'

'Don't know why you are getting so het up,' Carl snorted, 'it was only a black and they don't count for much.'

'I'm quitting this job,' Sandy cried, appalled. 'I didn't sign up for murder. They can hang you for that.'

Bones spoke quietly. 'They can hang you for rustling too, but you didn't make a fuss about that. You just took the money.'

Sandy stared at him. 'Killing a man is different. Even if he was only a black. He didn't have a chance against you.' Bones shrugged and turned his eyes towards the kid. Sandy looked into those dark orbs and shuddered. Something in the man's gaze terrified him. Bones smiled, a cold smile that never reached his eyes.

'You will do as you are told,' he whispered. 'Even if you don't agree with what we do, you don't argue. The only way you can show your disagreement is with a gun in your hand and you ain't ready for that, are you?'

Sandy swallowed hard and tried to bluster. 'Easy for you to talk, you ain't wearing a gun. You know I wouldn't go against an unarmed man.'

The thin man smiled again. 'I only wear my guns when I am ready to kill someone. Think yourself lucky I'm not wearing them now. Sit down and let's have no more talk of quitting. OK?'

Sandy sat and stared morosely into the fire. Bones sat up and stared at Carl.

'Right pretty vest you've got there, friend,' he murmured.

'Got it down in Mexico,' Carl explained.

'Have you always had a button missing?' Bones asked.

Carl dropped his gaze and swore. 'Where the hell did that go?' he cried.

Bones lay back again. 'I hope it wasn't when that black grabbed you to save himself from the fire,' he muttered. 'I hope you've got a spare, because if Eagles finds it he's gonna put two and two together. If I were you I'd either scrap the vest or sew another button on.'

Carl rose and crossed to his saddle-bag where he

rummaged and came up with a grunt of satisfaction and a shining silver button in his fist.

'I guess I'd better get sewing,' he muttered, and sat down again. The other two watched as he clumsily sewed on the new button. Finally he tied it off and held it up for inspection. Bones nodded his satisfaction; the kid said nothing, simply sat and stared into the fire. The other two looked at each other and Bones shrugged. The kid failed to notice the look that passed between his companions, he just watched the dancing flames. Finally he got to his feet and stomped around the small clearing.

'It's no good,' he cried. 'I just can't get that man's face out of my head. I've gotta get away, I just gotta.'

Bones looked at him and spoke softly, his voice full of sympathy. 'If you feel that bad about it why don't you take a stroll through the woods and try to clear your mind. Trees sometimes have that effect on folks. We'll wait for you to come back and discuss it then, OK?'

The boy nodded and walked out of sight; they could hear his passage through the undergrowth. Carl rose to his feet and stared after him. Bones said nothing.

'That kid's lost his nerve,' the big man stated. Bones nodded. 'Sooner or later he's gonna shoot his mouth off.'

'Probably sooner,' Bones concurred. 'Unless someone persuades him otherwise.'

'I'll give it a go,' suggested Carl and he turned towards the woods. Bones's voice stopped him.

'Take a shovel with you,' he suggested. Carl nodded and walked towards his horse. Bones watched as the big man left the firelight and followed the boy's tracks. He sat back and lit his cheroot. Gazing up at the stars he waited. Off in the distance a shot sounded and he smiled sadly. Carl's persuasion had worked, the boy wouldn't talk to anyone anymore.

After a while the big man came back, shovel under one arm, brushing dirt from his hands. Bones raised his brows.

'All settled?' he queried.

'I let the horse roam free; it'll get by 'til someone finds it. It's only a scrubby ol' cow pony anyway, ain't worth much. I buried his saddle with him.'

Bones nodded in agreement. 'Good! It don't do to leave too many traces. Now let's get some shuteye; we've got work to do tomorrow. We've gotta find Mr Eagles, wherever he is.'

CHAPTER TWENTY-ONE

They arrived at the Adler spread to find Gower and Laura inside the house. The burnt-out barn was plain to see as John sprang from his saddle, leaving Jobo to tend the horses. The girl leapt to her feet at his arrival and threw her arms around his shoulders. She sobbed quietly while he tried to console her.

'It's OK, Sis,' he muttered, as he stroked her back. 'Don't take on so. It's only a barn. We can soon build another.' His eyes met the sheriff's and read something in them. Laura broke away and the tall man spoke.

'It's a bit more than that, John. Eli was involved and whoever burnt down the barn killed him.'

'Killed? Eli? Why would anyone do that? He was just a grouchy old man. He never hurt anyone.' John was puzzled. Events had taken a different twist. No one had been killed before.

Gower shrugged. 'Maybe he recognized them. Who knows? Anyway he grabbed a clue for us to follow.'

Opening his fist Gower displayed a dirty silver button. John took it and looked closely.

'This looks like it's been burned,' he cried.

'We found Eli lying in the fire. This was clutched in his hand.'

John rubbed some dirt off it and gasped. 'I think I know where this came from,' he exclaimed. 'One of those three drifters wears a vest with buttons like that. I think we ought to pay them a visit.'

'Be right with you,' replied Gower. 'But I reckon we should bury Eli first. He wasn't a bad little guy.' The others nodded and they moved to the family plot. John selected a space just outside. To bury the man among white folks was, somehow, not proper. He began digging. Gower helped him to shift the soft rich soil. Laura called for the kid.

'Jobo,' she said 'Will you go into town and fetch the preacher? Eli was a religious man and deserves a good send off. Don't be too long, son.' Jobo, proud to be given a task, mounted his horse and disappeared off in the direction of town.

The two men dug a deep hole suitable to take the small body and rested a while. Gower looked deep into his deputy's eyes and asked the inevitable question.

'How did your investigation go, John?'

His friend paused awhile before replying. 'Pretty well, I guess. Someone has been driving certain landowners out and buying up their properties. The bank has been taking them for the mortgages they owe and then selling them on to another company. Those properties happen to be on the path of a proposed rail link from Maybeline – a rail link which has been abandoned but the property owner doesn't know that yet.'

'So someone is in for one hell of a shock,' Gower interjected. John nodded.

'The properties are held in the name of S&S Company. No more is known. But when I searched through the railroad's employment records a familiar name came out: Calvin Slavin worked there for a while during the extension plans.'

Gower whistled. 'That could explain the S&S part,' he muttered. 'Anything else?'

'You could be right,' mused John. 'The thing that bothers me is where he got the money from to buy those spreads. Even if his father helped him it would be difficult. A doctor doesn't earn a lot of money, most of his payments are in goods rather than money. You know what that means?'

The sheriff nodded. 'It means they have a backer somewhere along the way, someone with enough money to buy those places. Any ideas?'

'One or two,' John replied. 'I don't want to suggest anyone yet in case I'm wrong. Here comes the padre, let's get things over with.'

CHAPTER
TWENTY-TWO

Two drifters sat in the bar quietly drinking. The kid was not present but his absence was not noticed; drifters came, drifters went, so what? Carl was openly arrogant and staring at everyone who entered or left. Suddenly he grabbed a passing saloon girl and dragged her onto his lap. Her token squeals were soon subdued when he poured a whiskey down her throat and kissed her roughly.

'Come on, girlie,' he roared. 'Grab yourself some of this. It'll show what a real man is. If you've got a friend call her over, my *compadre* will be pleased to see her, I'll bet.'

'Fair enough, big boy,' cried the girl. 'If you've got the dinero Katie will deal you the goods. Hey, Katie, come over here and help this feller relax and spend some of his money.'

'I'd rather choose my own company, thank you,'

Bones's tone was firm and the approaching girl pulled a face.

'Please yourself,' muttered Katie. 'You don't know what you're missing.'

'I'll take that chance,' smiled the thin man. 'Another day I'd be pleased to oblige. But right now I'm busy.'

At that moment the door was flung open as the sheriff and John strode in.

'Stay right where you are,' Gower snapped, his gun pointed directly at Carl. 'That means everyone but you. You can stand up. Do it slowly and don't even think about going for your gun.' The big man obliged. John slipped behind him and slid the pistol from Carl's holster. He then moved around the front and gazed quizzically at the drifter.

'I was just admiring your fancy vest and its nice shiny buttons. How many buttons are there on it, I wonder? Ah, it looks like there are three.'

Carl sneered, 'Your counting ain't up to much, Mr Eagles. Last time I looked there were four. The same number as the buttonholes.'

John looked closer and spotted his mistake. A fold in the material had hidden one of the buttons. There was none missing.

'They are all here,' he stated. 'So where did that other one come from?'

'If we knew what you were talking about, Mr Eagles, we could maybe help you.' This was from Bones who had watched the whole thing with the usual grin on his skull-like face. The two lawmen looked at each other and Gower nodded.

'My barn was burnt and my farmhand killed,' stated John, coldly. 'Before he died he tore this button from the killer. As you can see it matches the ones on your vest.' He tossed the object on the table and three pairs of eyes watched it.

'Sure does,' Carl nodded. 'If you go South and cross the border you will find dozens of vests just like this one. If you want to pin a murder on me you'll need something better than that.'

Gower holstered his gun and spoke to his companion.

'Come on, John, there ain't nothing more we can do here. Let's get back to the office and think things through.'

Bones nodded wisely. 'That seems a good move to me, Sheriff. If you find any more evidence we'll be happy to help you. Any time, any place.'

John continued to stare at Carl. 'Someday you'll make the big mistake and I'll be there to get you.'

'You can try now if you fancy your chances, Eagles.' The big man smiled wolfishly. 'Why hang about? You have a big reputation but I ain't seen much to prove how good you are. Why not show me now?'

The sheriff's voice cracked out, 'There ain't gonna be no shootout in my town. Come on, John. We can pick him up later.'

John tore his eyes away from his challenger and turned towards his friend. 'Guess you are right, Chet,' he whispered. 'Rat killing can come later. We have important things to do right now.' He turned and walked out of the saloon, the laughter of Carl following him.

Bones spoke sharply to his man. 'Shut your mouth,

Carl. You ain't good enough to take Eagles in a straight fight and I need you alive. Later you can get your fool head blown off, but for now shut up.'

CHAPTER TWENTY-THREE

Back in the sheriff's office the two men were quiet. They had been outsmarted and it hurt. Chet tried to take his mind off things but he couldn't concentrate on the paperwork before him. His lanky frame was restless. John was no help, sitting across the other side of the desk, head in hands, lost in thought. Their reverie was interrupted by the entrance of Laura, still red-eyed from the funeral. Her brother stood and offered her his seat which she accepted.

'I can't believe anyone would do that to Eli. He was just a quiet little man, trying to earn a living.' Her voice was soft and John gave a sad smile. He remembered the reception the old man had given him. The term 'quiet little man' didn't seem appropriate, but he said nothing. Chet looked at her softly, his dark eyes filled with compassion.

'We'll get the critters, darling. I promise you that.' John was not so sure. They had been outwitted so far.

How long could it go on?

'He helped me when Ma and Pa died. He dug the graves and tended them. It was Eli who looked after the ranch for me. I know Brett helped me until Chet came along and took over.'

'Brett?' queried John. 'Brett Slavin? What did he have to do with it?'

The sheriff replied, 'Brett was carrying quite a torch for Laura. I think he wanted to marry her.'

She nodded. 'Somehow I just couldn't take a shine to him,' Laura stated. 'There was something strange about him. I can't say what it was but I could never have married him. I was grateful for his help but not that grateful. Then Chet came along and everything changed.'

John's eyes turned dreamy again and fresh thoughts came into his head.

'All this was after Pa died?' She nodded. 'How did Pa die? I never got that bit.'

'He was found at the back of our place with a gun in his mouth and his head blown open,' she replied. 'Obviously he had killed himself. He was never the same after Ma died.'

The gunman frowned. Something was wrong here; things didn't add up.

'Pa shot himself?' His amazement was in his tone. 'But he never owned or carried a gun. He hated them. That was the main cause of the trouble between us. He hated me learning to fire one. He'd never have shot himself. Who found him?'

'I did,' Laura replied. 'There was no doubt about it,

John, it's a sight I'll always remember. His hand was on the gun, finger on the trigger. His head . . . oh God, his head was. . . .' She broke off in tears and Gower crossed the room and took her in his arms, his body swamping her tiny frame as he glared at his deputy.

'Satisfied now?' he cried. 'What are you trying to prove?'

'I just want to sort a few things out,' John replied. 'Where was Doc Slavin while this was going on? It's important, Sis.'

She dried her tears and looked over Gower's shoulder.

'He arrived a short time later. He said he was on his way over to see Pa, he didn't say why. He just helped with the burial and stayed with me for a while,' she said, as John rubbed his chin thoughtfully. 'Is it important?' she asked.

'It could be,' muttered her brother. 'You've given me something to think about. Is that when Calvin came courting?'

She nodded. John rose and slapped on his hat. The sheriff stared at him.

'Where are you going?' he queried, still holding Laura. The other man smiled grimly.

'Just going to pay my respects to a couple of people,' he stated. 'I shouldn't be long,' and with these words he strode out into the evening air.

CHAPTER
TWENTY-FOUR

John arrived back at the stables just as the sun was paint-
ing the sky rose pink. The mountains stood out proud,
their rocky fingers pointing the way to the moon. He
tended his horse as Jobo was strangely absent and he
became aware of just how hungry he was. The scent of
hot food had tickled his nostrils as he rode past Mrs
Larriby's place and it was to there he headed.

The place was half filled with diners of many descrip-
tions: boys courting their sweethearts, couples having a
meal away from the kids, drifters, ranch hands. Mrs
Larriby was assisted by a younger woman, little and plain,
not too bright seemingly. As John entered, Mrs Larriby
herself hurried to serve him, her rangy frame seeming to
bristle with some inner excitement. She took his order
and then leaned forward to whisper in his ear.

'I'm right in guessing that you are John Adler,' she
queried, 'sometimes known as John Eagles?' He nodded.
'I'd appreciate a little of your time after your meal. It is

important.' Again he nodded.

'It would be my pleasure, ma'am,' he replied. She scuttled away barking orders at her waitress who seemed to be in a world of her own. John sat back in his chair and thought. What was happening now? Was it something to do with the present problem or some new pressure on his shoulders? He would just have to wait and see.

The meal was as delicious as ever, thick, juicy steak followed by smooth, mouth-melting apple pie. He leaned back in his chair and belched contentedly. The waitress came and shyly cleared his table. She leaned forward, displaying plenty of her ample cleavage and whispered, 'Ms Larriby says you've got to follow me out back. There's someone wants to talk with you.' He rose to his feet and smiled as he realized that even he was several inches taller than her, which gave him a sense of power for some strange reason. There were not too many people he could tower over, even his sister, Laura, was his equal in height. The girl pushed open the curtain and he followed her into a passage leading past the kitchen, into a large room which obviously served as an office, to judge by the account books spread over the table. There were three people already present: Mrs Larriby, the hotel owner Will Hardie, and Jobo. The boy grinned and rose to his feet. Hardie gave him a nod and Jobo disappeared out of the room. The hotelier beckoned John to a chair and sat opposite him. Mrs Larriby sat to his left and opened the conversation.

'I guess you don't recognize me, John. I don't blame you, it was a long time ago. Something over ten years since we last met. You were always a bright boy, a bit of a rebel certainly but with no real harm in you.' He looked closer at her, this scrawny woman he had barely noticed. Then he looked into her eyes, the eyes he had only seen on one woman before, large, lustrous and a glowing amber. The eyes of a mountain lion, the eyes of. . . .

'Miss Farriday,' he gasped. 'Good Lord! It's wonderful to see you again.'

'You were a very bright pupil,' she smiled. 'I never had favourites in my schoolroom but if I had it would have been you.'

Will Hardie grunted. 'Can we finish with the old town reunion? Let's get down to business. We all have work to do and Jobo isn't always patient.'

'Quite right, Will,' the old woman replied. 'We feel it's time you heard about what went on in this quiet little corner of hell we call Diablo.' John was surprised by her tone but said nothing. She tightened her lips and resumed.

'It all began about three years ago when the rustling and burning started. The ranchers and farmers around here have always got on pretty well. Neither of them interfered with the other and life was pretty quiet. Then certain ranches found their cattle disappearing. At first they blamed the farmers but found out that the farmers were suffering too, burnt-out barns and the like. Strangely enough not all were affected only those north of the river.'

John nodded. 'Those in a direct line to Maybeline,' he stated. The others looked surprised. He grinned and went on, 'I've been hired to investigate these things and that's why I've been away for a few days.'

Ma Larriby looked surprised and glanced at Hardie, who shrugged.

'Did you discover anything?' she enquired. John nodded.

'I found out that the railroad had planned to build out to here and those properties were in direct line. The railroad would have been paying plenty of dollars to buy that land. Whoever owned it would be very rich.'

'Schultz!' growled Hardie. 'I'm gonna have a few words with that *hombre*.' The gunfighter shook his head. 'The bank sold those properties to someone else. A company called S&S. I couldn't find out who they were but I can make a guess. Anyway it don't matter too much now, the railroad have changed their minds. They wouldn't make enough money coming this way, they are going east.'

'Someone is gonna be pretty unhappy about that,' grunted Hardie. 'I'd give my last dollar to see their faces when they find out.'

'That's all fine enough,' muttered the old lady, her tired eyes wrinkled in thought, 'but who did the rustling and burning and why wasn't your place included?'

'It's been included now,' replied John and told them of the earlier events.

They listened in silence until he'd finished then the old woman spoke.

'That's terrible news, John. Poor old Eli. You'd better catch them soon, son, they can't get away with that.'

'Yeah, I kinda took a shine to that old feller,' said Hardie. 'I know he didn't amount to much but he didn't deserve that.' They sat in silence for a while until the old woman broke it.

114

'We thought that the new sheriff was involved in the rustling. It seemed to start when he appeared and he hasn't been able to do anything about it, but now we're not so sure.'

'Has anyone been acting strangely around here since it all started?' John asked the question. 'Anyone been flashing a lot of money around or looking as though they know something no one else does?'

The other pair looked at each other and it was Hardie who spoke.

'Doc Slavin ain't been quite right since his youngest boy was shot. He ain't got any better since he gave up doctoring. Seems to be thinking of other things all the time.'

'He hasn't been right since your father died,' corrected the widow. 'They were pretty good friends for some time. When your mother died your pa found it very hard and it was Doc Slavin who pulled him out of it. We were all shocked when the suicide happened. No-one expected that. We all thought young Laura would marry Brett but then the sheriff turned up and things changed.'

'Tell me more about how Pa died,' John asked. 'I've been told some of it but it don't seem to ring true.' The others looked at each other again and, this time, it was the woman who spoke first.

'It didn't ring true to lots of people but the funeral took place and most folks forgot about it. A few of us older folk still wondered though.'

'I wasn't living here then but it didn't sound right to me either,' interjected the man. 'There were lots of questions that remained to be answered.'

'Will was a Pinkerton man for a while and knows a bit about crime.' The old woman's voice was low. John looked at Will Hardie with a new respect, the Pinkerton agents were well known as top class lawmen, equal to the Texas Rangers.

'What questions?' John asked.

'Why did a man who hated guns choose to shoot himself? There are other ways. Usually suicides leave a note, not always it's true, but generally. Why did he choose a spot where the shot could be heard so easily? None of the usual secrecy and privacy. Would he have done it within earshot of his own daughter? You knew him better than me, does it seem likely?'

John shook his head. 'He loved Laura too much to let her see that. Anything else?'

'There was a tintype taken of the scene. Tell me, was your daddy a southpaw?' John shook his head. 'Then from the picture taken he couldn't have fired the gun. If he had held it that way and pulled the trigger he would have hit the tree behind and only got a burn mark. I reckon someone shot him and made it look like a suicide.'

'Are you saying that Pa sat there and let someone push a gun into his mouth and shoot him? That's plain crazy.'

Hardie smiled grimly. 'Not if he was already unconscious when it happened,' he suggested.

The younger man sat and thought for a while. It began to make sense. The death of his father was no accident.

'OK!' he muttered. 'So the next question is, who

would do a thing like that and why?'

The woman leaned forward and touched his knee. 'We have an idea but can't prove anything. We've heard rumours and insinuations but they could be completely wrong. Henry Cantrell, the barber, claims that Doc Slavin was drunk one time and started shooting his mouth off about how he had fixed those damned Adlers. It may mean nothing, but on the other hand. . . .'

'But why?' John was puzzled. 'What could he get out of it? It was me he hated, not Pa.'

'I don't know,' confessed Hardie. 'We've just given you what we know. The rest is up to you.'

John rose and donned his hat. His brown eyes were thoughtful as he thanked them and left the room. He passed Jobo on the way and the boy started to say something but changed his mind when he saw the man's set face. Even at his age he knew when it was right not to speak.

CHAPTER
TWENTY-FIVE

There was plenty to think about as he walked away from the eating-house. Someone had killed his father, there was no doubt of that. Someone had put him to sleep, coldly blown out his brains and rigged it to look like suicide. Who would do it? Who hated him that much? Maybe it wasn't hate; maybe that someone wanted something and could only get it by the old man's death. What did Pa have that anyone could have wanted? Nothing . . . except the homestead. Maybe that was it. Whoever had bought up those other places would have needed the Adler spread to complete the line. Pa would never have sold out; he owed the bank nothing. His thoughts turned down another path: Brett Slavin. He had been keen on Laura. If she had married him the Slavins would have had control and when the railroad made its bid they would have been in the money. Could it be the Slavins behind this business? Buying the ranches from the bank would have cost a lot of money. He doubted if Doc Slavin had that kind of dinero. So what lay behind it? Who was backing him? The initials 'S and S' intrigued. If one 'S' meant 'Slavin', who was the other one? He only knew one other person, Abraham Schultz. That didn't make sense, the bank had sold the places to the highest bidder. It was getting very involved. A voice hailed him from across the street and he looked up to see the skeletal figure of the man called Bones.

'Ah, Mr Eagles. Can we have words please? It won't take long.'

John looked around carefully, the main street seemed empty and there didn't appear to be any signs of danger. He could see the figure of Carl looming in the doorway of the saloon, but he was simply lounging, presenting no threat. But where was the third man, the kid?

'I can assure you there is no threat to your life, I just want to talk,' Bones smiled.

'So, talk then.' John was curt, but cautious. After all Bones was unarmed.

'I come to offer you a little advice.' The voice was quiet, almost friendly. 'You are beginning to annoy certain people and that is unhealthy. My advice is to get on your horse and ride out.'

John raised his eyebrows. 'What if I don't?'

'Then, my friend, we will have to meet face to face and I will probably kill you.'

John looked at the man's gun free waist and frowned.

'Are you going to bore me to death?' he asked. 'Do I need to remind you that you aren't wearing a gun?'

'I wear one when necessary,' the other replied. 'When I do someone usually dies. Just think, Mr Eagles, we are probably the last real gunfighters alive. The best have all gone. Sooner or later we will have to prove something and I have the advantage.'

John stared at him. 'What edge do you have?' he asked.

'I've seen you in action, I know I'm faster than you. You don't know that I'm not.'

'Thanks for the warning,' John kept his voice calm. 'While we are chewing the fat here will you take a message back to your master?' Bones nodded. 'Tell him that things have moved along. The railroad have changed their minds. They don't think it's worth their while to extend to here. The plans are off.'

Bones nodded and with a final touch of his hat brim, turned away and walked back to the waiting Carl.

CHAPTER
TWENTY-SIX

The news was quickly circulated and Brett Slavin was ordered to wire the railroad company about the affair and then, if it were true, to tell the big man. For once he got it right and a meeting was soon arranged between Doc and the mystery man. There was a lot of gum beating until the dust settled and then all went quiet for a time until the hammer fell in the most alarming way.

The barber's shop was immediately across the main street from the bank and Henry Cantrell, who was locking up his premises, was the first to hear the shot. He hurried across the road and hesitated before the bank's main entrance which was, of course, closed. As he waited, the sheriff joined him and John Adler/Eagles came from the other direction. The three men gazed at each other, uncertain what to do. Cantrell pointed out the locked bank and John signed for them to follow him as he led the way round to the back office. This door was open and the trio filtered in. The gross body of the banker had slumped forward in his chair and blood was pouring over the top of his desk. His right hand still held the smoking gun. He was clearly dead.

'Cheeze,' The sound came from Jobo who had appeared from nowhere. Chet turned to him and told him fetch the undertaker. The boy scampered off. John approached the body and found a note which Schultz had written. He read it in silence and then passed it over to the sheriff. Gower read it and whistled.

'Jesus Christ!' he exclaimed. 'That explains a hell of a lot. After the body has been shifted we ought to have a pow wow.' John nodded, his brow still wrinkled in thought. Other townsfolk appeared now, drifting along in odd little clusters. Gower tried to disperse them. Eventually the undertaker appeared complete with wagon and the body was shifted. It took four men to carry the stretcher but eventually it was positioned on the floor of the wagon and was driven off to the funeral parlour. The crowd dispersed and the two friends walked back to the sheriff's office. They sat and looked at each other in silence for some time until Gower spoke.

'Well, I guess that answers a lot of our questions. We now know that Schultz was the brains behind the rustling and land deals and Doc Slavin was doing his dirty work. I guess the Slavin boys and those three drifters were involved too. Lets move in and get them.'

'You're the sheriff,' John remarked, shaking his head. 'But I guess I'd wait awhile. Doc Slavin is not a patient man and pretty soon he's gonna panic. He doesn't know about Schultz and if we keep quiet about the note, sooner or later he'll crack and do something stupid.'

Gower grinned and nodded. It made sense to him.

'Since we're the only ones who've have read the note I guess we have the upper hand. Let Doc play into our hands. We've plenty of time, let the jasper sweat awhile.'

'There is the problem with the bank,' John muttered. 'This note says that Banker Schultz stretched himself too far and my guess is that there ain't too much money in the safe.'

Gower stared at him. 'You mean the bank's busted?'

'That'd be my guess. I've got a feller I know in Maybeline, He's a lawyer but knows a lot about banking. If I send him a wire my guess is that he'd be here in a couple of days. His work with the railroad is finished and he's looking for something to do. How about I send for him?'

'If you reckon he'd come, go ahead.'

'From the way he was talking I figure he'd bite your arm off for the job. He has a wife and young family and figures it's time he put down some roots. He'll come for sure.'

Gower smiled. 'Well then, *compadre*, get yourself down to the telegraph office and send for him.'

CHAPTER TWENTY-SEVEN

John was proved right. When Slavin heard about the death of Schultz his first thought was self-preservation. He didn't regard either Gower or John as fools and realized that the whole scheme was falling apart. He summoned his sons and spoke to them firmly.

'We've got a lot of work to get through quickly,' he snapped. 'With that fat fool killing himself he's blown things wide open. We've got to grab what we can and get the hell out of here.'

The boys looked at each other and then back at their father.

'How does this make any difference to us?' queried Brett. 'It just means there is more money for the rest of us. That seems pretty good to me.'

Calvin agreed and the doc snorted.

'You half-blind idiots. God knows how I got you as sons, not a decent mind between the two of you. Maybe young Burt would have had more brains but Adler killed him.'

'Aw, Pa that ain't fair,' Brett complained 'Burt's death was an accident. The three of us were aiming at some cans and he ran across in front of us. That don't prove he had too much brain. Any one of us could have killed him.'

Doc rose to his feet, his skinny frame quivering.

'Everything that has gone wrong in my life is due to the Adler family. I could have married Ellen until Tom Adler stuck his nose in. She preferred a two bit sod scratcher to a doctor. I never forgave either of them for that. They made money while I was still trying to get my dues out of the people I treated and cured. Then lover boy here guaranteed that I could have the spread when he married Laura. That was fine until that young sheriff came along and spilt the wagon. Don't talk to me about the Adlers, if I say they killed Burt then that means they did and no one is gonna teach me different. Savvy?'

The brothers looked at each other and said no more. They knew better than to argue with their father when he was in this kind of temper.

'Now get out of here and let me think. Send that skinny drifter in, I've got work for him.'

Outside the brothers looked at each other. Brett, the younger, was openly scared. He had never seen his father like this and confessed his worries to his older sibling.

Calvin agreed with him, saying, 'He's been acting kinda queer since John Adler came back. I thought he'd forgotten all that rubbish about Adler killing Burt, now I ain't so sure. I never knew there was bad blood before; Pa and Mrs Adler, that don't seem right.'

'We'd better do something right,' suggested Calvin. 'Let's find Bones and tell him Pa wants him. I guess he'll probably be in the saloon.'

Brett shuddered. 'That man scares me,' he confessed. 'There is something about him that don't smell good. It's my guess that he would kill anyone if the price was right.'

'That's crazy,' Calvin scoffed. 'He doesn't even wear a gun. He's just a half-mad drifter with not too much brain. What's to be scared of?' Brett said no more but simply led the way over to the saloon where they found the pair leaning against the bar.

Big Carl was in his usual taunting mood. His smile turned to a sneer as the brothers neared.

'Hey lookee here, fellers. The two wonder boys are here. Guess they must have a message from their daddy, that's about all they're capable of. What do you want, children? New toys to play with? Let's see what we can do.' He began to laugh until the quiet voice of Bones stopped him.

'That's enough for now, Carl. Let's see what they want.' The big man was silenced immediately and lounged against the bar. He kept his mouth shut now but still kept the scornful look on his face. Calvin cleared his throat and spoke as bravely as he could.

'Pa wants to see you in his room as soon as possible. He's got a special job for you.'

The skinny man arched his brows and stood upright. Replacing his hat and squaring his shoulders, he walked towards to the door, turning back to look at Carl.

'Leave the boys alone for now, big man, we need them both. You can have your fun later. If I find either of them hurt when I get back, I'll kill you. *Sabe?*' The giant looked scared and nodded his head, all his arrogance gone as he turned his head to face over the bar. Bones grinned and left the saloon.

Doc Slavin's mood had not improved by the time Bones arrived. The tall man pulled up a chair and straddled it with his arms resting on the back. His skull-like face stared up at the smaller man insolently and a grin played around his thin lips. Slavin was boiling but held his temper in check.

'Took your time didn't you?' His tone was sarcastic.

Bones grinned wider. 'No one said I had to hurry,' he murmured 'Rushing isn't something I do a lot of. Anyhow, I'm here now. What do you want?'

'I want Adler or Eagles, or whatever name he happens to be using, dead. Stone, blind, dead, so that the whole pestilential family is gone out of my sight.' The doc's bile was pouring out now and he was slavering. 'My useless sons won't do it, I don't think your large friend can do it, so it's all down to you. I don't care how it's done, I just want him dead. Can you handle this chore, or have I got to do it myself?'

'Doc,' Bones kept his voice low and calm, 'it will be a pleasure. I've been wanting to prove myself faster than the great John Eagles and now is my chance.'

Slavin calmed down a little. 'Faster than John Eagles?' he gasped. 'But I've never seen you wear a gun.'

Bones grinned wider but his eyes remained cold.

'Oh, I wear a gun when necessary,' he whispered.

'One thing I can guarantee is that when I wear my gun someone is gonna die, and it might as well be John Eagles.'

Slavin sat down in his chair and breathed deeply. Something in this man's attitude assured him that the job would be done and he knew he could rest easier. His voice was calmer as he addressed Bones.

'This is what I want you to do.'

CHAPTER TWENTY-EIGHT

It was two days later when John met Bones. He had imagined that the thin man would have made himself scarce with the death of the banker, and yet, here he was, large as life sauntering along without a care in the world. He tipped his hat to the deputy and called out, 'Good morning, Mr Eagles, fine day isn't it?'

John stopped in his tracks. 'I thought you would have hit the trail by now,' he grunted.

The other man looked surprised.

'Why would I do that?' he asked. 'I'm just beginning to settle down here. It seems a nice friendly sort of place.'

'Suspicion of murder and rustling would move most people on,' the deputy commented.

'It's only suspicion. You can't prove a thing.' His smile never changed. 'Anyway I can't move on yet, I still have a job to do.'

'What job is that?' John asked. 'Or can't you tell me?'

'Of course I can tell you,' replied the other man. 'I've

got to kill you.'

John registered his surprise.

'How do you propose to do that?' he asked. 'You don't even carry a gun.'

Bones became serious. 'Oh, I wear a gun when I need it,' he explained. 'The next time we meet I'll be wearing a Colt. Then I'll kill you.'

'You sound pretty certain,' growled the other. 'Many men have tried before. What makes you different?'

'The difference is that I know I can beat you, and you don't know I can't. That gives me the edge. Have a nice life, while it lasts.' He moved past John and turned into Widow Larriby's place. John walked on towards the sheriff's office with his mind in a whirl.

The two friends were deep in discussion, seated each side of the sheriff's desk, with Gower's blue eyes locked onto John's brown. The indecision between them was clear.

'I don't see why we can't just go out and arrest them all,' John cried. 'The suicide note from the banker is enough evidence for me.'

'But not enough for the judge,' the sheriff explained. 'Nowhere is there any evidence that Doc and family were actually involved in anything illegal. They were with him in the land buying, but that ain't against the law. The three drifters could be anyone, although I believe it is Bones and his sidekicks. We've got to catch them red-handed with the stolen cattle, then we can do something.'

'Bring them in and get confessions later,' growled the other. 'That always worked in the past.'

'Times are changing, John,' Chet remarked. 'We've got law and order here now. We can't do what we used to.' he grinned ruefully.

'And dozens of lowlifes get away with murder,' John scoffed.

'I guess sometimes that happens but that's justice.'

'Then you can keep justice, I want revenge.' John stood up and removed the star from his breast. 'If I can't act inside the law then I'll act outside it.' He stormed from the room and Gower watched him go with regret in his eyes. He had a bad feeling about John's actions but knew there was little he could do about it.

He tried to turn his attention to the paperwork before him but couldn't concentrate. His mind kept churning over, Schultz, the note, Doc Slavin, the drifters, John and back to the Slavins again. He gave up on a bad job and, leaning back in his chair, closed his eyes briefly. The sound of the office door opening aroused him and he awoke fully to a soft voice whispering, 'Well, Sheriff Gower, so this is how you spend your time, dozing in the chair. I thought I was marrying a man of action, not a layabout.'

He opened his eyes to see the smiling face of Laura looking at him. He sat up, rubbed his eyes and blinked as he looked at his pocket watch. Two hours had elapsed since her brother had stormed out. He tried to establish some male dignity by denying that he had been asleep but the girl shrugged off all his attempts.

'I could hear you snoring from across the street. I wouldn't be surprised if half the town didn't hear it. I think I'll cancel our wedding. I can't live with a man who snores like that.'

'Aw, honey,' he groaned. 'I don't snore. At least no one has said so before.'

'Your lady friends must have been deaf,' the girl replied. 'I don't want to hear about your previous conquests.'

'I didn't mean that,' he wailed. 'There has never been any girl but you. I was talking about when I was trail riding on cattle drives. My pals never complained.'

She turned away from him and he stood, red faced and unsure what to do next. He was inexperienced with the weaker sex and couldn't see how to get out of his dilemma. He gazed at his fiancée's back and saw it shaking. Was she really that upset? Something about her movements didn't seem right. He heard muffled sounds and finally realized that she was laughing. Relief swept over him and he thought of how to exact his revenge.

'Since I seem to have picked up the snoring habit I wouldn't want to upset you. Maybe it would be better if we called the whole thing off.' He turned away as he said it and heard her laughter stop.

'What did you say?' she gasped. 'No, Chet, please. I was only joshing.'

He turned and faced her, and her expression was one of pure shock and fear.

'Only joshing, huh?' he growled. 'Well, maybe you were right: I ain't the man for you. No woman should be married to a snorer.'

'Chet!' she gasped. 'Please, you don't snore. At least you didn't then. Don't walk out on me. I love you. Please, Chet, don't do this.'

He picked up his hat and headed for the door.

'Too late, lady' he murmured. 'I'm going out to have dinner with someone who appreciates me, snores and all. A nice quiet dinner followed by a peaceful evening in great company.' He looked at her and grinned. 'Well, miss, are you coming with me or not?'

Relief rushed across her face and she hurried across and slapped his arm.

'You knew all the time,' she cried. 'You made me go through all that. I ought to slap your face.'

'You wouldn't want to bruise me for the wedding,' he gasped. 'What would folks think? The sheriff married to a husband beater.'

She laughed, linked her arm through his and they strode out into the evening air.

CHAPTER TWENTY-NINE

It was three days before John reappeared in Diablo and he wasn't alone. Riding beside him, and looking uncomfortable on a rangy bay, was his friend Lawyer Zach Lowcock. Both men had clearly ridden hard and their horses were dusty and blown. The pair dismounted outside the livery stables and John hollered for Jobo, who came running instantly. Both horses were led into the darker area of the stable where the boy began his work on them. The two men walked across to the sheriff's office where John introduced his companion.

'Chet,' he began, 'I want you to meet a friend of mine, Zach Lowcock. He's come along to look into the affairs at the bank and see just why Mr Schultz had to kill himself. Is that OK with you?' The sheriff shook the newcomer's hand and welcomed him.

'Nice to met you, Mr Lowcock. I ain't a financial man

myself and would appreciate any help there is. If there's anything you need, just yell.'

The lawyer smiled. 'You could start with the keys to the bank. I'd like to take a look at the books.' Gower reached into a drawer and pulled out a large bunch of keys which the lawyer took.

'Now, if you can just point me in the right direction, I'll make a start.'

The sheriff nodded and John led his friend to the bank from where he was summarily dismissed. He returned to the sheriff's office wearing a broad grin. Chet was waiting for him.

'Well!' he remarked. 'I'll say this much for your friend, he certainly seems keen.'

John nodded. 'He's one of the best men around. He'll soon find out what Schultz has been doing.'

'Sure hope you're right,' Chet murmured, in appreciation. 'I guess it's time to hit the hay. See you tomorrow, John.'

'Not seeing Laura tonight?' he asked.

The sheriff shook his head. 'She has some school work to do. It's good to have a break now and then. Don't leave it too late, son. You need your beauty sleep too.'

The deputy grinned and left his friend's office. The sheriff was right. A man could get too tired.

Even as they spoke, the object of their conversation was walking along the darkening street towards the livery stables. Born and raised in this town it held no fears for her. There were no celebrating cowboys from cattle drives around, Diablo was not recognized as a troublesome town and it was still quite early. The saloons had not started their evening entertainment yet and all was quiet. The lengthening shadows stretched across the street breaking the light into irregular patterns. The stables were in her sight where she knew her buggy would be ready, Jobo could always be relied upon. She thought she heard her name called, and paused in her stride. Looking around and listening she saw and heard no one. She shrugged and walked on, her imagination must be playing tricks. The voice came again this time much louder.

'Laura! Hold hard, girl, I want to talk with you.'

Now she could see a small figure in the shadows, a familiar shape she couldn't place at first. The figure moved and now she could see that it was Doc Slavin. She had always had a soft spot for the old man. She felt so sorry for him, he had lost so much over the years. She walked towards him. He smiled and took her arm.

'Thank you, my dear,' he muttered. 'I've got some news to give you that you might find interesting.' He led her behind the building, into deeper shadow. She didn't resist even when the darkness closed in. Finally he stopped and faced her. She waited patiently. The old man looked around and leaned towards her.

She heard nothing but two strong arms suddenly pinned her arms to her side and a rough hand was clapped across her mouth. Struggle as she might she could make no sound and was helpless in the iron grip. She kicked out with her booted feet and made connection with her attacker's shin. A snarl of pain resulted in a knee in the small of her back. The hand gagging her was

136

removed and instantly replaced by a smelly cloth. Her senses reeled and darkness closed in as she sank into unconsciousness.

CHAPTER THIRTY

Chet burst into the office where John was seated reading the latest mail. The sheriff was clearly agitated. Puffing and red faced he stopped and stared at his deputy. Finally he gasped out his message.

'Have you seen Laura?'

'Nope. Why? Is something wrong?'

The sheriff glared around and began pacing the floor.

'No one's seen her for a couple of days.' he growled. 'She hasn't been to the school; she isn't in her room, she's disappeared.'

'That's crazy talk,' snapped John. 'People don't just disappear. Maybe she went home. Have you looked there?'

The sheriff shook his head. 'Her buggy is still in the livery stable. Jobo said he had it all ready for her two nights ago but she never came for it. I guess she wouldn't have walked there, it's too far.'

John was beginning to share his friend's fear now as he rose to his feet.

'We'd better start looking around,' he said. 'Someone must know something.'

The two men took different parts of the town and met up later. Diablo was not that big a place and the search didn't take long. The deputy had learned nothing, but Gower was holding something in his right hand. John looked at it and his blood ran cold.

'It's Laura's purse,' he gasped. 'Where did you find that?'

'In the alley between the barber shop and the gunsmith's,' replied the other. 'Someone has got her, John and we've gotta find out who. Did you question everyone in your section?'

John nodded. 'The Slavins weren't in and the barber was at work but everyone else was accounted for.'

'I spoke to the barber,' the sheriff stated. 'But where the hell are the Slavins?'

'Their name seems to be popping up everywhere,' growled the other. 'If I catch that evil old crow I'll wring the truth out of him.'

'Unless I catch him first.' The sheriff's tone was cold and boded ill for the old doctor.

Before they could move very far the tall figure of Zach Lowcock entered.

'Sorry to interrupt, folks,' he began. 'I figured you'd like to know what I've found out. The banker was deep in trouble; he'd spent the bank's money on the gamble that the railroad was coming through here. When he realized it wasn't, he knew he was finished. There was no way he could pay the money back and he couldn't expect any financial help from his partners – they weren't that friendly, it was a business deal not a friendly society. The properties are held in a company called S&S Holdings.' The first 'S' was Schultz himself and the other was someone called Slavin. Ring any bells?'

John whistled. Slavin again.

The lawyer continued, 'I can get busy sorting out the bank's affairs and will run it until it's back on it's feet, if that's OK.'

Both men nodded approval and looked at each other. John whispered one word, 'Slavin!'

'Mr Eagles.' John whirled round and saw Jobo standing nearby. 'I want to tell you about the last time I saw Miss Adler.'

Both men stared at him and then at each other. The sheriff had not involved the boy very deeply in his enquiries. Jobo hesitated and cleared his throat.

'I had the buckboard ready for her to drive home and when she didn't come along I looked out and saw her walking up Main Street. Then she stopped and seemed to be talking to someone in the alley down aways. I couldn't see who it was but I could see that it was a man.'

'What were they talking about?' asked Gower.

The boy looked sheepish. and dropped his gaze.

'Dunno! They was too far away. I could just hear her voice and a deeper one that sounded like a man's. She walked into the alley and I never saw her again.'

John leaned forward and asked. 'Is that all you saw?'

The boy shook his head. 'I didn't know what to do so I waited a while. Then a man came out of the alley and walked towards his horse. Mr Eagles, it was Doc Slavin. He rode out of town heading east and soon after a buckboard followed him. There was a kinda bundle on the back and that's all I saw.'

The two men looked at each other again and said together, 'Slavin!' They thanked the boy and sent him off clutching a shiny dollar in his hand. John's temper was up as he glared at his friend.

'The sooner we speak to one of the Slavins the better. They got a heap of explaining to do.'

Gower nodded. 'What are we waiting for? Let's get moving.'

'On your way, friends,' urged Lowcock. 'I'll take care of things here.'

CHAPTER
THIRTY-ONE

Laura Adler sat in the chair facing the door. She had no alternative because there were strong bonds tying her there. Her dress was torn and dirty and a filthy cloth covered her mouth. She could still feel the grimy hands that had clutched at her breasts on the journey to this remote cabin and she was scared about just how far the Slavins would go. She sat in terror with the tear streaks marking her cheeks. She had never felt so helpless in her life. Somewhere out there the two men she loved most were risking their lives for her and she could do nothing to help them. She wriggled slightly and the torn dress fell away from one proud, rose-tipped breast. The bruises from groping fingers and slobbering lips stood out clearly under her pale skin. She could still feel the creeping horror of the last few hours and Doc Slavin's words rang in her ears.

'Remember, boys, the one who kills Adler gets the woman to play with as he likes. She will be the last of the plague of Adlers and the world will be better for that. But you've gotta be good. Do what you like to her, but don't go beneath the waist; that pleasure will be reserved for the man who kills Adler, savvy?'

She remembered the crude laughter and comments that had followed and fresh tears filled her eyes. Why was the doc doing this? What had he got against her family? As though to answer her queries the doc himself came through the door and sat facing her, his arms along the back of his chair. His eyes were thoughtful as he looked at her and there was a strange look in them, rather like a fire glowing in the darkness of the black orbs.

Reaching across he slid the gag down over her chin. He appraised her and read her intention in her eyes.

'Scream all you want, lady, there ain't nobody around to hear you, 'cept maybe your brother and that will only draw him closer so we can kill him quicker.' He lowered his gaze and appraised her naked flesh before he spoke again. 'I never realized just how much like your mother you are; almost as beautiful as she was. Yes siree, you sure are bringing back all kinds of memories.'

'What do you know about my mother?' she snapped. 'What can her looks mean to you?'

He grinned rather ruefully. 'Your mother was the only woman I ever loved,' he replied. 'I courted her for a long time until your father came along and stole her from me.'

'You . . . and my mother? I don't believe it?' Laura gasped.

'I don't give a goddamn what you believe,' he shrugged. 'It's the truth. We had an understanding until

143

Adler spoiled it. I married the next woman who came along but I still carried a torch for your ma. Every time I saw them together I felt sick. Then she had you kids and that was even worse. Over the years my hatred of your family has grown. Then your precious brother had to go and shoot my youngest boy. How would you have felt?'

'But that was an accident,' Laura cried. 'There were three boys firing guns when Burt ran across the range. Any one of them could have killed him, even his own brothers.'

'Adler killed him,' roared the doc. 'Whichever way you look at it my boy was dead and your brother was there. That's an end to it.' Laura said no more and the old man continued in a quieter tone, 'Then there was you.'

'*Me?*' queried the girl. 'What have I done?'

'My son, Brett, tried to court you but you didn't want to know. He wasn't good enough for you. Even when your mother died you stayed cold and hard to him. That is why I killed your father.'

'You killed my father? Why? He was your friend.'

Slavin laughed. 'That's what the stupid fool thought. His friend? After all he'd done to me? All he owed me? Friend! He made it all so easy. That last night, some time after your mom was gone, he came and started blubbing like a baby. I tried to console him and offered him a drink. It was easy to slip a little powder in it and he went to sleep like a good little boy. Calvin and me took him out into the woods and sat him under a tree. I put the barrel of my gun into his mouth and blew his brains out. Then I just fixed it to look like he'd done the shooting.

144

We left him there for someone to find. Easy!'

He sat back grinning and watched fresh tears run down Laura's cheeks. His eyes roamed over her body, the dishevelled hair, torn dress and whole picture of help-lessness roused feelings in him that he hadn't felt for a long time. Even a man of his age could still feel yearn-ings. He leaned across and touched her bare breast. He grinned when he felt her revulsion. This little filly needed breaking in and if his two remaining sons weren't up to it, he'd take on the job himself. Yessiree, it could be a long night for young Laura.

Finally he left her to sit and think about what he'd said. He had killed her father. For so long they had appeared to be friends, but now Doc Slavin was showing his true colours. She remembered his earlier remarks about giving her to the man who killed John and shud-dered. The actions of these animals had revolted her. The big man, Carl, was a monster, he had grabbed, bitten and slobbered over her body like a wild beast; Brett was shy and gentle and had whispered his apologies as he kissed her ears. Calvin had been clumsy and coarse, trying to outdo the others but the worst one was Bones. She had never met anyone as cold and expressionless as him. His fingers on her flesh had felt like the claws of a bird of prey. His eyes, oh God, would she ever forget those dead green eyes that promised her hell. She knew that if he won her she would die screaming in mortal terror before he could do anything and she hoped it would be the case. For now, all she could do was sit and wait.

There was the sound of voices in the other room and

Slavin was clearly in a foul temper. The other man raised his voice in protest which she recognized as belonging to Brett Slavin, the younger son.

The door opened and the doc stormed in, red faced and with thunder in his eyes. Brett followed and tried not to look at Laura seated across the room.

'I don't care what you say, Pa, it just ain't right. Laura is a lovely girl and she's done nothing to deserve this. I don't hold no torch for Adler but he ain't really done me no harm. I want no part of it.'

'You stupid fool!' his father sneered. 'No part of it? You are in it up to your neck. If you want this girl fer yourself you have to kill her brother. I'll give her to you gift wrapped. Just do what you are told.'

Brett shook his head. 'I really loved her, still do, but not like this. I don't want any part of that. You want me to commit murder and rape and I can't do it. Just think, Pa, they can hang you for both those things. I am getting out while I can.'

Doc modulated his tone and this frightened Laura even more. He had never seemed so dangerous.

'Aw come on, boy, you're too deeply involved now. Remember they can hang you for rustling, and that didn't seem to bother you too much. It's too late now, it's gone too far to stop. Stick with me, son, we can get out of this. Trust me.'

Brett shook his head again. His eyes were full of tears as he gazed at his father.

'I'm sorry, Pa, but I can't stay. Come with me; we can start again someplace where no one knows us.'

The old man shook his head. 'If you feel that badly,

boy, then you had better go. Get out now, I won't hold it against you. Find yourself a new life, with my blessing.' He extended his hand and his son clasped it before breaking away and turning towards the door. Doc smiled coldly, drew his pistol and shot the boy through the back of his head. Walking across, he dragged the bleeding corpse outside and dumped it in the dust. He came back to the room still smiling that strange smile. He walked towards where Laura sat and began talking in a strangely sweet voice.

'That's better, Ellen, now we're alone and can get to know each other better. No one can interrupt us now.'

She realized then that Doc Slavin was quite mad.

CHAPTER THIRTY-TWO

The trail was easy to follow; too easy, Eagles thought, it was as though Slavin wanted to be found. Doubts crept into his mind and he tried to relay these to the sheriff but Gower wasn't listening. The woman he loved was at the end of this trail and he wasn't prepared to wait for anything. He reluctantly agreed that John should follow his own way and that they would meet up where Laura was imprisoned. John wheeled his horse and turned off the trail. His path was grassier than the previous one and he frequently left the saddle to survey the terrain. Finally he found what he sought, a slight trace of smoke in the distance. It didn't look like a camp-fire and yet there were no buildings here that he remembered, only an old miner's cabin, long deserted and falling apart. Stealthily he inched his way forward until he overlooked a shallow valley. Rocks surrounded the dusty trail and now he could clearly see the figure hidden in one of the many crevasses that scratched their surfaces. He saw the figure rise and throw a rifle to its shoulder. John unsheathed his Winchester and levelled it. His skill with a rifle was not as great, but he felt he could do what was necessary here. The figure of the sheriff, still mounted, rounded a bend and, as the bushwhacker squeezed his trigger, John fired.

Two things happened at once, Gower's mount screamed and fell and the gunman was hurled back into the rocks by John's bullet. The sheriff was still alive, John could see that with a glance, but his leg was trapped beneath the fallen steed. The assassin had disappeared and that worried John.

The deputy moved carefully, well aware of possible trouble, the bushwhacker was unlikely to be alone. In a final scrambling rush he dashed to the fallen sheriff. Gower's horse was dead and now its weight was trapping its rider's leg. Taking care to shelter himself behind the dead beast John took stock. The sheriff was still alive to judge by his language, but he was in severe pain from his trapped leg.

'Where the hell were you when I needed you?' he growled.

'Busy saving your worthless hide,' he replied, grinning. 'I couldn't let my sister marry a man with too many holes in him. Now, where are you hurt?'

'The bullet got the horse, but I figure the fall broke my leg. If you can get this mustang off me maybe we'll find out for sure.'

Moving the corpse was no easy task, but, eventually, their combined strengths succeeded in freeing the fallen man's leg. He lay there, bathed in sweat, ashen faced and John completed an examination of the injured leg. It didn't need a trained eye to show that it was shattered, the white gleam of bone was enough to prove that. Looking down into his friend's face John said. 'I guess I do the rest of the job myself. Just lie here and enjoy the scenery, it shouldn't take long.'

He scrambled away from the prone body of the sheriff. Every nerve was stretched to breaking point. An expert in his field he felt no sense of fear, just the strong urge to survive which had kept him alive in many tight situations. Everything else was pushed to one side, Gower, Doc Slavin, even Laura, were peripheries to be thought about later. For the moment all that existed were the hidden killers and himself. As he dashed towards the cover of the rocks he heard the sound of movements above him: a careless boot scratching for a foothold, a chink of metal striking rock. Someone was nearby. He stopped and listened again; nothing, and then when he thought he had imagined it, he saw the sudden flash as the sun caught bright steel. His eyes were focused but his other senses were still alert for noises or smells. He grinned when he heard the growl of a dog. His sidekick had come back, just in time for action.

He waited, and watched until he heard what he wanted to hear, a snarl, a cry of pain and sudden silence. Then a startled voice cried out from the left of his hiding place.

'What the hell was that? Can you hear me, Slavin?'

'I don't think he can hear you, Carl. He has problems of his own.' John's reply was not well received, as a curse and a pistol shot came in reply. John took a chance that Bones was present and called on the big man's ego.

'I thought you were a gunfighter,' he taunted, 'and I'm just a blowhard. Why not come out and prove yourself a man? Or maybe you're just a yellow cur.' As he spoke he stepped to one side and waited.

'I'll show you who's yellow,' screamed Carl as he leaped from his hiding place with his six-gun blazing. John grinned and shot him in his tracks. There was no need to examine the body, he knew it was dead.

Winchester in hand he began circling the rocks until he was above the cabin. John could see no sign of life. He took a pair of ex-army field-glasses from his saddle-bag and looked closer. The body lying just outside the door was Brett Slavin's. He breathed easy and replaced the glasses. The dog had accounted for Calvin Slavin, someone else had killed Brett, the kid, Sandy, had left the scene and that left only the doc and Bones. It was the last name that worried John, he was the danger man. He rose gingerly to his feet.

'Where the hell are you, Mr Bones? Where are you hiding?' he whispered to himself.

CHAPTER
THIRTY-THREE

Slavin was so entranced by what he was doing that he didn't hear the door open, or see Bones stuffing a wad of bills into his jeans pocket. The thin man coughed and attracted some attention. The doc tore his hand away from Laura's breast. Bones had the usual grin on his skinny face and his eyebrows lifted as Slavin glared at him.

'A gentleman would knock before bursting in,' snarled the doc and Bones's grin grew wider.

'I ain't never been called a gentleman before,' he replied. 'I don't know too much about them. Would they be messing about with girls young enough to be their daughter?'

Slavin went white with anger but knew better than to tangle with this man. 'What do you want anyway?' he demanded. 'I thought you'd be out helping the others.'

Bones scratched his nose reflectively. 'Ain't much help I can give to dead men,' he muttered. 'I figured I'd better grab my own irons and get ready to deal with Eagles myself.'

Slavin's jaw dropped. 'Dead?' he gasped. 'All of them?'

'Most all of 'em. Carl is holding out but I don't give much hope for him. Your boy, Calvin, has lit out for places unknown.' The lie came easy to his lips, he could feel the wad of money in his own hip pocket.

'He wouldn't run like that,' said Slavin, vehemently. 'Even he had more guts.'

Bones pursed his thin lips. 'You'd know him better than me. I only know he cleaned out that cash box of yours and hit leather and he sure enough wasn't heading towards the fighting.'

Slavin dived across the room and grabbed the cash box he had been hoarding for weeks. The thin man was right: it was empty. The old man's head reeled, his boy, to do this to him. A sudden rage took hold of him and he snatched up his rifle. He grabbed Laura by the hair and dragged her towards the door. Bones watched as he buckled on his gunbelt.

'Where the hell are you going?'

Slavin called back over his shoulder, 'This young lady is gonna see her brother die.'

'Fair enough,' replied Bones. 'But I aim to do the killing. It's what you hired me for.'

'Then get on with it,' snarled Slavin. 'I'm gonna watch to make sure you do.'

The skinny man slowly checked his gun and finally strode towards the door. He looked down and stepped over the body lying just outside.

'Seems neither of your boys could do right by you,' he sneered. 'They paid idiots to kill Eagles and both failed. Damn good job you hired a professional.' With this remark he walked off towards his horse and swung into the saddle.

'See you out there, *compadre*,' were his last words as he rode off.

Slavin swore at his disappearing back and, still pulling Laura by the hair he forced her into the buckboard where she lay sprawled in the back.

'Come on, lady,' he snarled. 'One way or the other you are about to see your brother die.'

Eagles looked around, all was quiet and the sheriff lay where he had been left. Carl's final shot had taken its toll. He had been hit in the shoulder and was in obvious pain. John took a chance and knelt beside him. Chet tried to grin through tight, gritted teeth.

'I guess I ain't helping too much,' he said 'but you seem to be coping pretty well. How many are left?' John pursed his lips.

'Far as I can work it out, probably two. Doc Slavin and Bones and it's Bones I'm more worried about.'

Gower thought awhile and then stated, 'I heard a gunshot off in the distance a while ago. Maybe only one is left.'

'I don't think I can take that chance,' he mused. 'Brett has been killed by one of those two and now I'm worrying where Bones is.'

'Bones is right here, Mr Eagles.'

John looked up quickly to see the skeletal figure

standing quietly before him. A quick glance revealed the six-gun at his hip. Bones was grinning.

'I thought it would come down to us two. The other Slavin boy crossed his daddy and paid the price so we won't be disturbed. The doc is someway behind so we can finally test each other.'

John stood up slowly and faced his foe.

'Anytime you feel lucky, my friend,' he stated flatly.

'Luck isn't going to come into it. It's down to your speed against mine. Make your play.'

It seemed an eternity before either man moved, eventually John broke the silence.

'When the whippoorwill sounds again,' he suggested. Bones nodded and they fell silent once more. Finally the tiny bird, encouraged by the stillness, burst into song. Two hands flashed downwards and two guns spoke as one. Gower had never seen anything so fast. Both men stood still for a brief period and then Bones fell backwards, blood spurting from his heart. He was followed by his opponent, who tumbled on to his back suffering from a stomach wound, both hands clutching his gut and blood spurting between his fingers. Gower could see he was mortally wounded, but at present was still alive. He was helpless to assist, his shattered arm and leg ruled him out of the picture. He was still clutching his rifle although it was empty of shells. Then Slavin appeared.

He was dragging Laura by her hair. The girl was in agony and unable to do much as her hands remained tied. The doctor was swinging his rifle in his free hand and sneering at the fallen men.

'I knew it was stupid hiring fools to do men's work. I

might have known it would come down to me. That's OK though, it's only right and proper that I should be the one to finish off the rats' nest called Adler.' He grinned down at John who was trying to reach his fallen gun. With a derisive kick he sent the weapon spinning over the edge of the rocks. He gazed at the sheriff who had thrown his useless rifle away. He saw no threat from either man and started to gloat.

'You, Adler, are gut shot and will die soon enough, the sheriff will meet his fate soon after, but first I'm gonna have me a little fun with the young lady here before she dies too. Both you boys can watch; it might be the last thing you both see.'

He released Laura's hair and grabbed her around the waist. He dropped the rifle and pulled her to him. His free hand grasped her neck and he crushed his lips against hers. Struggle as she might she could do little against his surprising strength. Finally he broke away and let his hand fall to her bare breast. She squealed as he crushed it and lowered his head towards it. Suddenly her booted foot shot out and caught his shin. He yelped and released her, cursing as he did so. His right hand flew out and smashed her across the face. In fury he snatched up his rifle and aimed it at her head.

'You damned spiteful bitch,' he roared. 'You are more like your mother than I thought. Right then, lady, you can die first.'

His finger whitened as he took up pressure on the trigger and then another gun, from behind John, roared and the old man fell like a sack of potatoes. In astonishment John and Gower looked at each other and then came realization as Jobo's voice cried out. 'I got him, Mr Eagles, I got him.'

John smiled through his pain. He looked at the boy's face and saw the shock of taking a life reflected upon it.

'You did good, son,' he answered. 'Now go and untie Miss Laura's hands, take my horse, he's yours now, ride into town and bring back help.' The boy nodded and hastened to obey. John laid his head back and closed his eyes.

CHAPTER THIRTY-FOUR

The dog was worried; something in his head was telling him that things were bad with the man he loved. He remembered his last orders but was torn by instinct. He glared at his prisoner and crept towards him. The boy cowered and a whimper escaped from his lips. He was utterly defenceless, his gun lay out of reach and the shot from Eagles' gun had shattered his shoulder. This brute was going to kill him and he could do nothing. He could sense the sharp teeth tearing and ripping his life away. He was hard against a rock, there was nowhere to go, he just had to wait. The dog picked up the fallen gun and dropped it over the side of the cliff where it smashed against the rocks. With a final backwards glance at his prisoner the dog disappeared among the rocks.

Calvin waited with bated breath but, eventually plucked up courage and dashed to where his horse was tied. Without a glance back he leaped into the saddle and headed out. There was no way he was going to tangle with Eagles or that beast again.

The dog stood on a high rock and stared down. He could see the bodies lying around but was only concerned with one. The boy was struggling to untie the girl and so the dog crept down to lie beside his friend. The sheriff called a warning but the boy, with a quick glance explained, 'It's OK, it's Mr Eagles's dog. He won't hurt him.'

The dog laid his head on Eagles's chest and licked his cheek. John opened his eyes and smiled.

'I guess you will be travelling alone now, old pardner. I won't be around to look after you. Watch out for those bears.' The dog rose and slumped away, head down, drooping tail, looking the picture of sorrow.

The trio watched him go as Jobo freed Laura and ran off towards John's horse. The dog paid them no attention, just slunk off into the rocks and sat in its own form of grief.

John closed his eyes; the pain had gone. Laura gazed at him with tear-filled eyes and saw him smile, a soft, gentle smile, full of love and happiness. He spoke just once. He uttered one word, 'Nita', and died.

EPILOGUE

They buried him quietly in the family plot with his parents and brother. There were only a few people present, a solemn faced priest, Mrs Larriby and Hardy, The barber, Henry, and Jobo accompanied a tearful Laura and the sheriff, right arm in a sling and walking with a crutch to save his broken leg. Zach Lowcock and Sarah made up the numbers The service was short, the headstone bore a simple message just the dates of his birth and death, his name and the words:

John Eagles/Adler
Who finally came home.

John Eagles had found the peace he always craved and his days of looking over his shoulder were over.

The dog watched from the brow of a hill and, when the last mourner had departed, he howled his grief to the setting sun and trotted off to the safety of the mountains.